DEMOLITION DAD

Also by Phil Earle, for older readers
Being Billy
Saving Daisy
Heroic
Bubble Wrap Boy

Phil Earle

DEMOLITION DAD

Illustrated by Sara Ogilvie

Orion
Children's Books

First published in Great Britain in 2015
by Orion Children's Books
an imprint of Hachette Children's Group
a division of Hodder and Stoughton Limited

Orion House
5 Upper St Martin's Lane
London WC2H 9EA
An Hachette UK Company

1 3 5 7 9 10 8 6 4 2

ISBN 978 1 4440 1386 3

Printed in Great Britain by Clays Ltd, St Ives plc

www.orionchildrensbooks.co.uk

I wrote this book for Raymond William Ernest Earle - the Hulk Hogan of dads. The greatest, the champ, the best of all time.

I'd also like to dedicate it to my friend Sarah H, who would probably make a lousy wrestler, but is one heck of a fighter...
P.E.

For Chris, Carolyn, Kyle, Katie and Matthew
S.O.

Who's Who in Storey Street...

Jake

Dad

Mum

Lewis

Flass

Mouse

Masher

Arnie McBride

The Terror

Working Nine to Five

Jake's dad was a Demolisher.

There's no other or better word for it. No word that could make Jake prouder. From nine to five, Monday to Friday, Jake's dad took buildings from the clouds to the floor, sometimes in the blink of an eye.

There was no one smarter, quicker, or better at it than George Biggs, which was just as well, because there were lots of buildings in the seaside town of Seacross that were, frankly, an eyesore, a carbuncle, a green pus-filled wart on the face of the landscape.

Dad had been a builder once; a good one too, apparently. But that was before people had stopped coming to Seacross on their holidays in favour of a week toasting themselves in the Costa Del Hot. When the tourists dried up, so did Dad's building work.

Jake thought his dad deserved to be rich and famous for what he did. He thought crowds should gather to watch him, cheering as he climbed the crane's ladder, whooping when he took the front of the building clean off with a single glance of his wrecking ball.

But no one ever watched George at work apart from Jake (peering through the fence) and he couldn't understand why. It wasn't as if there was anything else for the people of Seacross to do. After all, George had destroyed the crumbling old cinema three years ago.

And the bingo hall.

And the art gallery.

The leisure centre had collapsed on its own (though that's another story).

Yes, Jake was George Biggs's number-one fan, the proudest son in the history of demolishers' sons, probably ever. The greatest days were the ones where he was allowed to squeeze into the crane's cab with his dad, wedged between his bulging gut and the controls. On special occasions, like his birthday, he was even allowed to manoeuvre the wrecking ball into action, his dad's pudgy sausage fingers wrapped softly over his. It was moments like this that made Jake want to burst with pride. Only the thought of cleaning the mess off the crane window actually stopped him from doing so. I mean, can you imagine the mess?

To everyone else, George might have been fat and balding, with a ponytail as bushy as a shire horse's mane, but Jake knew something that everyone else didn't. And he had a plan. A secret sort of plan. So secret, even HE didn't know how it worked. Not fully. He doesn't find out for a good few chapters yet. But bear with him. It's well worth it when the penny finally drops.

You see it wasn't just buildings that George Biggs demolished. Oh no. At weekends, he knocked other things down. And that's when Jake got REALLY excited, because once this secret was out, everyone would know how amazing his dad was.

He could hear the crowd now, jumping to their feet, chanting louder and louder as Dad hoisted Jake victoriously onto his shoulders . . .

DEMOLITION MAN . . .

DEMOLITION MAN . . .

DEMOLITION MAN . . .

DEMOLITION MAN!

2

The Weekend Job

Tinny music poured through the speakers and the crowd went bonkers.

Well, I say a crowd – that depends on your definition of the word. If a crowd to you means three hairy truckers, two bored businessmen, a gaggle of gummy old women, and a pair of teenagers snogging each other's faces off, then yes, this was a crowd. A BIG one. It certainly was to Jake. He'd been to shows where a lot fewer people turned up – and quite a few when the only person applauding and going mad was him.

No – tonight, the atmosphere was electric, and as the familiar theme tune rumbled around the sports centre walls, Jake felt the hairs on the back of his neck stand on end, just as they always did. No matter how many times he heard it.

The music was familiar because Jake had written it on his laptop, on one of those fancy app thingies: a swirling mixture of rolling drums and thrashing guitars – the perfect way of introducing Dad to his legion of fans.

Jake knew that right now Dad would be hiding behind the curtain, costume on, biceps oiled and flexed as he leaned into the microphone, waiting for the guitars to screech to their peak.

'Laydeeez aaaand gentlemeeeen.' His voice exploded over the speakers, causing a hysterical hiss from the hearing aids in the audience. 'Readying himself for the ring is the Master of Disaster, the Eighth Wonder of the World, the King of Sting, the one, the only, De-mo-lit-ion Man, GEOOOORGIIIIE BEEEEEEEEE!!!'

The microphone howled its approval and the tatty black curtain bulged to reveal Jake's dad in all his weekend glory.

Six foot five and twenty stone of Man Mountain, swinging a rubber wrecking ball round his head, and decked out in a tatty black leotard which barely kept his rampaging belly under control. At his feet, an old desk fan blew his ponytail out behind him.

Jake whooped his approval, fighting the chorus of boos from the pensioners.

There he was, the Demolition Man, the wrestler everyone loved to hate. Well, everyone except his son.

George threw his hands in the air. He pointed menacingly at the grannies, threatening to break their Zimmer frames for the disrespect they were showing him. Only when he saw Jake ringside did he let the persona slip, winking slyly before straddling the top rope and removing a slice of cold pizza that had been thrown – *splat* – between his shoulder blades. Instead of throwing the pizza back into the crowd, the Demolition Man grinned and yelled over the noise.

'Pineapple on pizza is a crime! I ordered pepperoni!' With a mock grimace, he picked off the offending fruit and flicked it to the ground, before folding the entire slice into his gaping mouth.

The crowd lapped it up, and so did Jake. Dad was used to having things thrown at him on his ring walk – it happened a lot to wrestlers as they made their dramatic entrance. Pizza, boiled sweets, beer bottles – Dad had once even had to remove a pair of false teeth from his bum cheek after a particularly aggressive grandma got overexcited. She'd never got her gnashers back though – they were sitting in a shoebox under Jake's bed, along with other souvenirs from Dad's wrestling career. Ticket stubs, flyers, an eyebrow ripped from Pretty Boy Brian's head. Each object was precious to Jake, more loved than any toy he'd ever owned. One day, he knew, there'd

be a museum in Dad's honour. There'd be exhibits and plaques, statues made of solid gold . . .

Jake took a deep breath. He was getting carried away. Dad had only been wrestling at weekends for about a year, after all. But as for watching it together? That had been going on for as long as he could remember – he and Dad would snuggle on the settee to watch fights. It was their special time, after Jake's little brother Lewis was tucked up in bed and Mum was relaxing with a book. They'd laugh, boo and shout at the TV:

'Did you see that move, Dad?'

'I did, son, I did.'

'He won't be able to sit down for a week after that!'

'Not without a rubber ring, no.'

Once the programme had finished, they'd play-fight, re-enacting their favourite moments.

By the time Jake was eight, he couldn't help noticing the similarity between the hulks on the screen and the one next to him on the sofa. In fact, Dad was bigger and tougher than most of them put together. How amazing it would be, Jake thought, if it was his dad up there, strutting his stuff. So amazing, Jake decided, that it HAD to happen, and he started to put a plan into action.

'You should be a wrestler, Dad.'

Dad laughed. 'Me? I don't think so, son.'

'Course you should. You'd squish everyone they put it front of you.'

Dad growled mock-fiercely, before hoisting Jake one-handed above his head, and up the stairs to bed.

But Jake knew Dad was destined to wrestle, even if Dad

didn't, and he took every opportunity to tell him so. He drew pictures of Dad in costume, came up with an alter ego and a finishing move for him; he even found a wrestling organisation advertising for new fighters, and printed off dozens of application forms, leaving them in Dad's pockets, under his pillow – even, once, inside a sandwich. Mmm, tasty.

In the end (and after a nasty bout of indigestion), Dad got the message.

'But *why* do you want me to wrestle?' he said.

Jake stared at him, incredulous. Why couldn't Dad see what he did?

'Are you kidding? You're the strongest person I've ever met. You're already the best demolisher in town. So I know if you body-slammed anyone in the world, well, you'd be the best at that too. And then I'd be even prouder. The proudest!'

Well, that was it. When your son thinks that about you, there's only one thing you can say.

'Grab your coat then, Jake. If I'm doing this, I need you in my corner.'

And so the Demolition Man was born, though he came with one simple rule:

'All of this stays a secret,' Dad said. 'Our secret.'

'Oh.' Jake felt a pang of disappointment. If Dad was a champion wrestler, he wanted *everyone* to know about it.

He thought quickly.

'But we can't keep it a secret. What about Mum?'

Dad looked thoughtful and a little bit scared.

'Hmmm. Good point. We'll have to tell her. Not that she's going to like it. No one else, though. Deal?'

Bummer, thought Jake, before having another brainwave. 'What about Lewis?'

'OK, Lewis too.'

'But he'll never keep it quiet. We might as well tell everyone.'

'No!' insisted Dad, his eyes as stern as a headmaster who's caught you nicking his favourite sweets from the tuck shop. 'No one except family can know. Not even Mouse and Floss.'

'But, Dad!' Jake said. 'I don't understand why it's such a big deal. Jack at school boasts about how good his dad is at football all the time. Why do I have to hide this?'

'Because Jack's dad doesn't appear in public dressed in Spandex, does he? Nor does he have to cover himself in baby oil before a big match.' Dad dropped his voice, as if suddenly worried someone over the sea in Holland might hear him. 'And besides, Jack's dad is a bit . . . well, thinner than me, isn't he?'

'That'll be your secret weapon, Dad. Look at the world champion on the telly, the Tsunami Terror. As soon as he sits on someone, that's it. Game over!'

'The Terror doesn't have to spend five days a week on a site with fifty mouthy builders. If they saw a photo of me in a leotard, I'd never hear the end of it. Plus there's your mum. Can you imagine her face if she thought the neighbours knew I spent the weekends jumping about in Spandex? She'd never live it down! No, that's it, Jake. That's the promise we make here and now. No one except Mum and Lewis can know – or we give up before we begin. Deal?'

Jake bit his lip. It wasn't perfect; far from it, but they had to start somewhere.

'Deal,' said Jake, shaking on it, keeping the fingers of his other hand crossed behind his back.

He wouldn't tell a soul. Oh no. No way.

At least, not yet.

3

Scalping The Slasher

It was Saturday. Wrestling day, Jake's favourite day of the week, and he was spending the morning the same way he always did – loading up Dad's van with objects of demolition.

Not sledgehammers or crowbars – they were for weekdays only – no, this was something entirely different.

'One ironed leotard – check!' said Jake happily.

'Knee supports – check.

'Wrestling boots – check.

'Rubber wrecking ball on elastic chain – checkity-check!'

Jake didn't really need a list to remind him what to pack. He knew it off by heart. He just liked doing it. He also knew that he had to prepare the props without giving anyone the tiniest hint of Dad's alter ego.

But Storey Street wasn't an easy place to keep things under wraps, and even this early on a Saturday morning, there were plenty of people about.

Jake had lived on Storey Street all his life. He liked it too, mostly. The way everyone knew each other, not in a nosy-peeking-through-your-curtains kind of way, more a stopping-burglars-nicking-your-laptop kind of way.

It didn't matter if you lived in the posh red-brick semis at the farm end of the road, or the dilapidated old terraces in the shadow of Jake's school (like he did), everyone knew each other. No one passed each other in the street without a 'morning', 'wotcha' or 'how do'. Half of the kids in Jake's class lived on the street, including his two best mates, Floss and Mouse, and that was the way he liked it.

It did, however, make packing the van a tricky proposition.

'What *are* you doing?' came a voice from behind him. Mouse. He and Floss were perched on their mountain bikes, backpacks full of food, heads full of adventure, hoping that Jake might join them for once.

'Nothing,' said Jake. He pretended to yawn and spread his arms wide to block his friends' view. 'Just loading Dad's van.'

'Duh, obviously,' chirped Floss. 'But why?'

'Helping him on site, aren't I?'

'On a Saturday?'

'Buildings don't knock *themselves* down, you know,' Jake said.

'Fine,' said Mouse, with a sigh. 'Your loss. We're going down the docks. Rumour is they've found the hull of an old pirate shi— Hang on . . . is that a real wrecking ball in there?' He frowned. 'It looks a bit . . . rubbery.'

'Course it's real,' snapped Jake, slamming the doors. 'I can prove it, if you like, by wrapping it around your lug-holes!'

That got a laugh. Jake, Floss and Mouse had known each other since their bikes had stabilisers. They knew everything about one another. Well, almost everything. Jake wanted to tell them about Dad, more than anything. He wanted to tell the whole world. But Dad trusted him, and he couldn't let him down.

He watched as his two best friends cycled away. Then, feeling slightly wistful, he turned his attention back to the task in hand.

After a few more minutes of intense concentration, a shadow fell over him. It was only when Jake spun around that he realised it wasn't a cloud blocking the sun. It was Masher Milner and his sidekicks, Saliva Shreeve and Bunions Bootle (attractive boys, both).

If there was one downside to life on Storey Street, it was living near Masher. Lots of roads come complete with a Masher. You know the type: a hulking, insensitive meathead, with fists like cement and a desire to make people's life a misery. Especially people like Jake.

It was like having his own twenty-four-hour personal bullying service. Like all bully boys, Masher had an entourage. A bit like pop singers always carry little rat-like dogs in their handbags.

'Hey, look, it's Dork Boy, son of Fat Man,' said Masher. He was *always* going on about Dad's size.

Jake tried to respond, but it was hard to talk with Masher's fingers up his nostrils. He concentrated instead on trying to imagine Dad body-slamming the bully from a great height.

'What've you got in there?' Masher asked, wiping his fingers on Jake's shirt.

'Just Dad's stuff for work . . .' stuttered Jake.

'What? His packed lunch, is it?' he laughed. 'You're never going to fit it all in there. You'd need a bus!'

'Yeah, a double decker!' Saliva guffawed.

'So where are you off to today then, Biggs? A national pie-eating contest?' said Bunions.

'Or are you taking Daddy shoe shopping?' Masher was in his element now. 'Must be years since that lard-ball tied his own laces.'

'Or even saw his feet,' added Saliva.

Sides were starting to split.

'I heard that your dad is SO fat, when he falls over and cuts himself, gravy comes out!!'

That was it. All three of them almost lost control of their bladders, and Masher clambered into the van.

'Get out!' Jake screamed. 'There's private stuff in there!'

Then something weird happened. The sun disappeared *again*. Masher turned with a frown as Tropical Storm Dad broke all over him.

'WHAT ARE YOU DOING IN MY VAN, YOU TOERAG?!' Dad raged so ferociously that Masher and his guard dogs turned into a pack of scaredy-cats. Gone were the taunts and insults. They whimpered something about looking for a lost ball before scampering away down the street.

'What was all that about?' Dad asked.

'Oh, nothing.' Jake beamed proudly at Dad. Ha! If Masher was scared now, imagine what he'd be like if he saw Dad in the ring! He wouldn't dare bully him then.

When the van was loaded and the equipment ticked in triplicate, Dad and Jake were off over the hills to tonight's venue, a sports centre (though sometimes it was a bingo hall, or church). Wherever there was a ring and a cowering opponent, the Demolition Man would fight in it. And he never left defeated.

'Who's tonight's mug, I mean, opponent, Dad?' said Jake.

'Slasher "the Barber" Gash.'

'Oh yeah, of course. Good name.'

'Good persona too,' said Dad. 'Shaves the head of anyone he pins to the canvas.'

But Jake wasn't worried. He'd done his research. Knew Slasher's weaknesses.

'He's not all that. Don't forget he works to a budget. Those clippers of his aren't even cordless. How can he beat you when the nearest plug socket is in the dressing room, forty metres away?'

'Maybe he's got an extension lead,' Dad said, grinning.

'Or some garden shears.'

'Need more than that to cut through *this* hair,' Dad said.

Jake believed him. He knew how today's fight was going to go.

The crowd would boo, Dad would snarl and the bell would ring.

The Demolition Man would prowl forwards, full of menace, with one thing on his mind. Inflicting pain.

There was only going to be one winner. the Demolition Man would be going home with his ponytail intact.

4

Chicken Bones and Golden Beards

Jake should have been tired on the journey home, but he wasn't.

He never was after watching Dad wrestle.

Instead, he sat in the front of the van and relived every moment of the fight, while Dad speedily emptied a king-size bag of Cheesy Balls.

'It was amazing,' Jake said. 'The way you teased him with his clippers. He was so scared he was on the verge of cutting his *own* hair off!'

Dad grinned, his bushy beard golden with the dust of a thousand cheddary snacks. It made him look lion-esque, which suited him. After all, he was the King of the Ring.

'And what about the final move, eh, Jake?

Just the way we planned it?'

'Are you kidding me? It was perfect. Slasher didn't even touch the top rope as he flew over.'

Jake loved the way Dad finished off his opponents. More than he loved the outrageous costumes, boisterous ring walks and trash talking put together. Because Dad always dispatched his foes with his signature move, the Wrecking Ball, a whirling, swirling whoosh of the forearm that spun faster than a helicopter's propeller. And when that arm made contact flush on the chin? It was as if they'd been whacked by Dad's crane.

THAT'S how devastating it was.

'I hope Slasher's all right,' Dad said, stifling a yawn. 'It took the kiss of life from that old dear to bring him round.' The yawn turned into a shudder. 'Pass me them chicken legs, will you? I need something to take my mind off snogging grannies. It's killing my appetite.'

Jake rummaged in the hamper and found six fried chicken legs packed among a mountain of sausage rolls, and chocolate bars, as well as a bag of rotting lettuce, which had been there so long that it was beginning to look more like seaweed. Smelled like it, too.

Dad shuddered at the sight of the green stuff, before snatching it from Jake and throwing it out of the window, triggering the angry horn of a car behind.

'I don't know why your mum insists on buying that muck. She knows I'm allergic. Does funny things to my belly.'

'What, like making it smaller?' joked Jake.

'Exactly,' said Dad, sucking the meat from a chicken leg in one swift breath. 'And we can't have that, can we? Not when we're on a roll.'

The van went quiet. Jake thought about what Dad had just said. Something special was happening with his wrestling. He *was* on a roll. But not enough people were seeing his skills and Jake couldn't help but want more than a crumbling sports centre and an audience with an average age of eighty-nine.

'Dad,' Jake said. 'Wouldn't you enjoy it more if the crowd was bigger and noisier? I mean, imagine a sea of people on their feet, screaming your name again and again . . .'

Dad didn't reply. He had a faraway look in his eyes, and for once Jake didn't think he was fantasising about food. He needed to keep the conversation going. Make Dad see his way of thinking.

'So,' he continued. 'Who do we fight next?'

'I don't mind. Whoever they put in front of me.'

Jake thought hard.

'Problem is, I don't think there's anyone on our circuit who can pin you – fifty fights and no one's even put you on the floor yet!'

'All it takes is one blow, son, and all that can change. Any fighter can lose. What makes them a real champion is how they get up again. You hear me?'

'Of course.' It was a line Jake had heard many times before.

'Besides, there are plenty of good fighters out there. Ones we shouldn't write off.'

'Like who?'

'Giggles Maguire.'

'You're kidding me?' Jake said, laughing.

'No, he's dangerous.'

'He's a clown. A kids' entertainer.'

'So?'

'Who wears his mum's make-up!'

'And?'

Jake sniggered. 'And his signature move is choking opponents with balloon animals!'

'Like I said, he's dangerous.'

'But, Dad, if he puts his giraffe anywhere near your beard, it'll burst. He's hardly a threat, is he?'

Dad thought again.

'The Earthworm, Eddie McGraw.'

'You'd squash him flat, no problem!'

'The Wrestling Reverend.'

'You'd make him eat his dog collar!'

'Fat Boy Freddie, then. He's fearsome.'

Jake shook his head. 'Didn't you hear? He's had a gastric band fitted. Doctor's orders. Lost fifteen stone and taken up flower arranging. Apparently he has a real flair for it.'

The van fell silent, except for the sound of chicken legs being devoured. Dad was out of ideas, which left Jake to come to the following conclusion: there was no one who could beat his dad – he was untouchable, the greatest. The best of all time.

But what was the point in Dad being the greatest if only he and a few grannies knew it?

Jake slumped in his seat, and watched as Dad effortlessly sucked the meat from another chicken leg.

If the Demolition Man was going to get the recognition he deserved, it was up to Jake to do something about it.

5

The Exits are Here, Here and Here...

Not everyone shared Jake and Dad's love of wrestling.

Jake's mum, Lucie, hated everything about it, especially Dad's involvement.

'You're doing *what*?' she'd gasped when Dad told her. 'What on earth are the neighbours going to say?'

'They might be impressed,' Dad said hopefully.

'Impressed? They'd be impressed if you finally fixed the front wall, or cut the grass once in a while. I hardly think the sight of you in a leotard is something they're going to be dazzled by.'

'Look, it's just a bit of fun. Something for me and Jake. No one else has to know. It'll be a secret between the four of us.'

Mum sighed dramatically, before giving her reluctant seal of approval.

They'd met long before Dad became a wrestler, before the beard, ponytail and belly (his, not hers), when Dad was still an athletic builder, *laying* bricks instead of ripping them down.

Years ago, Mum had been an air hostess and met Dad while serving him on her very first flight. Dad, feeling smitten, asked her for the most expensive gift on the trolley and, after coughing up his free peanuts in shock at the price, bought a *three hundred pound* bottle of perfume, which he gave straight back to her. The smoothie. And that was it. They were a couple. (Though Jake had heard the story so many times that he'd learned to close his ears whenever they told it, concentrating instead on listing in his head every wrestling champion since the year of his birth to stop himself from throwing up.)

Mum wasn't an air hostess any more. Jake and his little brother, Lewis, had stopped all that. Instead of jetting all over the world, sampling the delights of Rio, Hong Kong and Benidorm, she was in charge of a crumbling old house and two demanding boys, sampling leftover fish fingers and stewarding piles of dirty washing.

Jake knew Mum missed her job. She hid it well, but he knew anyway. Every night, she'd tell them the best stories imaginable. She never read them from a book though; she told them straight from her head. Tales of faraway lands, places she'd visited, stories she'd learned especially for them. She told them with such passion that Jake and Lewis were transported to India or China, Italy or France – wherever that night's adventure came from.

Jake loved these tales, though he couldn't help noticing, despite Mum's smile, that her eyes were sad. As if telling the stories was a reminder of what she was missing.

And it wasn't just at bedtime that Mum acted, well, a little strangely, if Jake was honest. In the mornings, when he and Lewis raced downstairs for breakfast, she would greet them at the bottom of the stairs with a huge smile and a hug, just like any other mum. But lately Jake had started to notice that she seemed a bit overdressed for a day of washing and ironing.

She would flash a smile and say a squeaky 'Good morning!'

before pointing them towards the kitchen table, as if they didn't know where it was.

'Please take a seat,' she'd exclaim. 'Breakfast service will begin shortly.'

She wasn't lying either. While other mums would leave cereal boxes on the table, Jake and Lewis's mum arrived with a gleaming trolley, loaded with variety packs of cereal. (Never the Choco Pops though – Dad always ate those first.)

'Can I offer you something from the trolley?' she'd ask, which always made Lewis laugh. But Lewis was six.

Jake loved his mum, but this was a bit . . . well, odd. He didn't need serving; he could pour the milk himself. He would have preferred her just to sit and talk to them, like mums did on the telly.

He never said anything though; he didn't want to upset her. Because if Mum was upset? Well, he wouldn't be allowed to watch the wrestling on the telly, which was nearly as important as watching Dad on a Saturday.

'Why don't you go outside and play?' she'd ask.

Jake would frown. Where was the fun in that? He couldn't *play* wrestling, not when his favourite TV fighters always told them, 'Kids, we are trained athletes, who practise even in our sleep. Please don't try this at home.'

No, Mum didn't understand. And she saved her real feelings on the subject for Dad, who often got an earful when they thought Jake was asleep.

'All I want, George Melvin Biggs (she always used his full name when she was cross), is a holiday. Is that really too much to ask? Is prancing about in fancy dress *really* that important?'

'Well, it's difficult. I have commitments,' Dad said.

'Commitments?' she raged. 'COMMITMENTS?! Too right you do – commitments to this family.'

'People have paid to watch me fight! I can't let them down—'

'*Them*? Be honest – how many people actually make up *them*?'

Dad stammered. (Thank goodness he never dithered like that in the ring! Jake thought.) 'Well, it's hard to say. It depends on the venue—'

'I'll tell you how many people will be disappointed,' said Mum. 'Ten. A dozen, at most. And most of them are so old, they could be cheered up with a game of bingo and a plate of soft food.'

'There's Jake in all this too, remember.'

'I'm thinking about Jake. That's the other reason we need a holiday. All this Spandex and grunting isn't good for him. He needs a break from it. Heaven knows, we all do!'

Dad flashed a killer smile as he pulled Mum into a hug. 'And I'll give you a holiday soon, I promise. I'll take you to the moon and back one day.'

Jake didn't like this sort of conversation. He heard it on a weekly basis, though somehow Dad always managed to hold firm, and the holiday never happened, which was a relief. I mean, imagine a week in a leaky tent, with no telly and NO WRESTLING!

They couldn't afford a break. Not when the Demolition Man was in the form of his life. Jake had to keep looking for that next opponent, for a victory that would convince Dad to go public, to become the wrestling superstar he deserved to be. He had no idea how close he was to that moment but, believe me, he was about to find out.

6

The World of WOW!

It was a normal day in the Biggs's house. Jake was watching wrestling on the telly with Mouse and Floss, who had been round for tea.

It won't surprise you to hear that Jake was the only one *really* watching it. Mouse was reading his seventh comic in twenty-four hours, while Floss hunched over her laptop, editing the latest

movie she was working on, a zombie flick called *One Eyeball Left*. She'd tried to persuade the boys to star in it, but hadn't been too disappointed when they'd refused. People always said not to work with children or animals and, between them, Jake and Mouse fell into both of those categories.

'Did you see that?' gasped Jake, as the Tsunami Terror slammed another opponent straight though the ring.

'Amazing,' said Floss, eying her screen with admiration.

'Brutal,' said Mouse, staring at a panel in his comic.

Jake didn't notice. As far as he was concerned, his friends LOVED the grappling as much he did. Who wouldn't when the Tsunami Terror was fighting on screen?

WOW! or *World of Wrestling!* was a weekly round-up, beamed straight from the US of A, full of the biggest stars and deadliest moves. That's why Jake loved it. There were no children's clowns or bored vicars fighting here – only the maddest, meanest and muscliest maniacs from all over America.

WOW! fighters had the greatest identities, nearly as dramatic as the Demolition Man himself. There was:

THE SKYSCRAPER – RANDY O'FINIGAN

THE BLING-KING – PADDY RITZY

And DAVEY CRASHMAT McNASTY.

But none of these could match up to the mysterious and downright lethal Tsunami Terror, who had arrived from nowhere a year ago and proceeded to dispatch every wrestler put in front of him with his signature move, the Ten-Ton Tidal Wave. Jake had never seen anything like it. The Tsunami Terror was big – like HUGE. He was fat, but not flabby. He didn't wobble as he walked, though the ground appeared to shake beneath his every

step. He could've used Jake as a toothpick and made Dad look pretty enough to be in a boy band. He always arrived in the ring the same way – no thundering music or snarling walk through the crowd for him.

Oh no.

The lights would snap off dramatically, only to return ten seconds later, to reveal the Terror towering in the middle of the ring, eyes closed and arms outstretched. He wore a leotard of the royalest blue with a wave crashing across it. On his chest was a tattoo which spelled out a single word – DOOM. To finish off the ensemble was a mask that covered his entire head. Silvery hair poked from underneath, along with a series of mysterious-looking scars. The sight of him was enough to have opponents running for the exit. And his signature move, the Tidal Wave? Imagine 200 kilograms of breezeblock flying towards you from the top rope, with a roar so terrifying it should belong in the slobbering jaws of the world's wildest beast.

Jake loved and feared the Terror in equal measure; would watch through his hands as victims were stretchered from the ring, almost feeling the living-room floor shake as the wrestler roared his disapproval at another weak opponent.

'Is no man strong enough to withstand the Tidal Wave?' the commentators would gasp.

'THE DEMOLITION MAN IS!!' Jake wanted to yell, but he knew there was no point. No one from *WOW!* would hear him. America was too far away. And anyway, he'd promised to keep Dad's wrestling a secret, and he wouldn't go back on his word.

Tonight, though, was different. It was as if Father Christmas, the Tooth Fairy and the Easter Bunny had all clubbed together to give Jake the best gift ever. For, just as the programme came to an end, Arnie McBride, the Head of *WOW!*, popped up on screen. An ex-wrestler himself, McBride was the man who made *WOW!* tick, the man who organised the fights every fan wanted to see. He was a legend! His teeth glistened like pearls as he grinned at the camera and spoke straight into Jake's eager ears.

'*WOW!* fans from around the world. We need you. I need you. And I need you NOW!'

Jake shivered in anticipation as the great man went on.

'Are you MAN enough to rise to this challenge?' he asked in a voice that was pure gravel and grit. 'Could you be the next *WOW!* superstar and make your debut at Grapplemania? Could you be the one to end the reign of the TSUNAMI TERROR? Well? Could you?'

Jake's brain scrambled in excitement. Grapplemania? There was no bigger date in the wrestling calendar. The night when a hundred thousand fans packed into one stadium to see the greatest fighters battling it out. Millions tuned in around the world. Jake reckoned they probably even watched it up on Mars.

This was it – fate. Jake bounced off the sofa, pulling Mouse into the deadliest headlock ever witnessed on British shores.

His friends looked at him in a mixture of wonderment and terror. Well, Floss did. Mouse was floundering like a fish as his lungs emptied of oxygen.

None of them were looking at the TV any more. None of them noticed the message that appeared in the tiniest print at the end of the ad:

WOW! will not accept responsibility for injury, death or anything worse that results from taking part in this wonderful, once in a lifetime competition. See our lawyers for details

Not that it would have mattered to Jake if he *had* seen it. He was blinded by the opportunity. It was as if the competition had been designed especially for Dad. It would finally show the WORLD that Dad was the greatest demolisher, the greatest wrestler and the greatest dad on the face of the earth.

This was his time; Jake's time too. If he got things right, he knew there was no way that he, or his unsuspecting dad, could possibly fail.

7

Secrets and Lies

Laughter bounced around the walls like one of Dad's opponents off the ropes.

Jake winced. It wasn't the volume that hurt his ears, it was the *way* they were laughing.

'Hang on a minute,' Mouse said, guffawing. 'You're telling me your dad's a . . . wrestler?'

Jake nodded.

'Does he have one of those stupid names when he fights?' said Floss, giggling.

'Yeah, yeah, laugh it up. He's the Demolition Man: the best fighter out there. Honestly, you should see him in action. He's been unbeaten for over a year!'

To prove his point, Jake yanked his phone from his pocket and pulled up some footage. The others gathered round to see Dad send the Librarian of Mercy flying over the ropes. It was such a savage example of the Wrecking Ball that Jake could have sworn the phone shuddered in his hand.

'Whaddya make of that?' he said, beaming.

'Picture quality isn't great,' Floss said, with a frown. 'You should've borrowed my camera – it has an integral flash.'

'What is he *wearing?*' scoffed Mouse. 'If he's meant to be some kind of superhero, then he's failing miserably.' He held up his comic and pointed at Daredevil's slick red outfit. 'Now *that's* a costume!'

'OK, so it's a bit rough around the edges, but look at the skills he's got. No fighter lasts more than five minutes in the ring with him and they're running out of opponents fast. But this competition,' Jake pointed to the TV, '*this* could change everything. If Dad beat the Terror at Grapplemania, he'd be world champion, and that'd mean fighting all over the world. In front of millions! Everyone in town would see how brilliant Dad is. He could take Mum on the holiday she wants. You could come too. We could hire a jet, a mansion in the Hollywood hills with a pool and everything! We can do this. We *have* to!'

Mouse and Floss looked at each other.

'*We?*' Mouse said.

'But we *hate* wrestling,' said Floss.

Jake stared at them. Hate wrestling? What?

'Sorry, but we do,' said Mouse. 'It's just a bit . . . well . . . lame.'

Jake bit his tongue so hard he tasted blood.

Lame?

He was about to list all 173 reasons why wrestling was the greatest and toughest sport in the world, when he realised there wasn't time. There would be millions of applications for the competition, and Dad's needed to be the best.

'It doesn't matter,' he said. 'You don't have to watch. I just need your help . . . please?'

His friends looked at one another and smiled. Jake was their best friend.

Plus, it wasn't as if Seacross had anything more exciting to offer.

'Why not?' they replied together.

Jake smiled. This was it. Game on.

Dad looked confused. Baffled. Mystified. Like a man who'd been asked to cut his toenails with a hairbrush.

'It's not that I don't like the new costume,' he said, with a frown. 'I just don't understand what's wrong with the old one.'

'There's nothing *wrong* with it,' said Jake. 'It's just a bit, you know, tired. But this one? You look like a superhero. You could be BATMAN!'

The smile on Jake's face was so large it practically stretched past his ears. Though it wasn't an entirely genuine one, because he was nervous.

Dad did look cool, course he did, but he wasn't daft either. If he got even the slightest whiff of something funny going on, Jake knew the costume would end up in the bin.

Dad turned in front of the mirror, looking over his shoulder. A superhero, eh? He could buy into that.

The new costume was a *huge* improvement. It had needed
to be, too – Jake's thorough inspection of the competition rules
showed that each entrant had to submit a video of themselves in
action and in full battle gear. There'd be no auditions or knockout
rounds – Arnie McBride would choose the next *WOW!* superstar
from the comfort of his air-conditioned office.

And there was only one person Jake would trust with the
important task of Dad's new look – Mouse, the superhero fan
boy, expert in super-cool costumes.

At nursery, where Jake had first met him, Mouse was never
without his Superman outfit. In fact, it was only in Year Four, after

a run-in with Masher, that Mouse had stopped wearing the cape over his school uniform. (Jake was pretty sure Mouse still wore it under his shirt, tucked into his pants, but it wasn't a question you could ask. Not even of your best mate.)

Yes, Mouse had pulled off a blinder with Dad's new kit. It was still a leotard, but the design now included a vibrant collage of bricks, with a wrecking ball smashing across Dad's belly. The way his gut wobbled as he walked made it look like the ball was actually moving, knocking the wall down. It was pure theatre!

Mouse had added see-through sleeves, with fake tattoos plastered from shoulders to fingertips. There were images of explosions and dynamite all over his biceps and forearms, plus *BOOM* and *BOMB* etched into his knuckles. Truly epic stuff.

To top it off, there was a mask in matching red, with the same brick design and 'DD' stamped upon it. Dad looked more fearsome than he ever had in his life. Here was a man who could stand toe to toe with the Tsunami Terror. One bump with his belly would be enough to put the *WOW!* champ straight on his butt.

Jake caught Dad mock-snarling into the mirror, fingers curled into fists. He knew then that he had his approval. It was time to launch into Phase Two.

'Brilliant!' he said, whipping out Floss's camera. 'Do that face again.'

Dad didn't look so fierce when he saw the camera's red light winking at him.

'What are you doing? Where did you get that camera from?'

'What, this?' Jake said, innocently. 'I borrowed it from Floss.'

'Floss? You didn't . . .' George's huge bushy eyebrows arched in irritation. 'I hope you haven't told her. That was the deal. . .'

Jake's forehead felt hot. He knew not telling Dad about the competition was wrong, but he also knew that if he did tell him, there was every possibility he'd say a big fat no. And he couldn't risk that.

Jake tried to look shocked. 'Of course not! I've borrowed the camera for a school project. And anyway,' he stammered, quickly changing the subject, 'you look awesome. Your opponents won't know what's hit 'em.'

'Well, make sure you delete them photos then. Straightaway. No downloading them, you hear?'

Dad turned back to the mirror and smiled.

Jake relaxed and knew he'd done enough to throw Dad off the track.

The new costume was a keeper.

Jake lifted the camera and Dad raised his fists. He growled like a pit bull who'd just been called a poodle by a very sarcastic cat.

'That's the way, Dad,' Jake said. 'Do that again. Once more, like you're about to squash the Terror flat!'

How do you Demolish a Stoat?

So began a new reign of destruction. A reign so powerful that Jake wondered if Mouse had made Dad's new costume from Superman's cast-offs.

Dad was a man possessed, disposing of his opponents with such brutality that Jake almost felt guilty recording it all. Not that he had a choice. Floss had given him *very* clear instructions on how to film each fight: when to zoom in, when to cut away, when to focus on Dad, when to linger on his opponent's expression of terror.

Nothing could get in the way of the plan now. They had three weeks until the competition closed. That meant three weeks to compile a five-minute show reel so packed with demolition that *WOW!* would have no option but to make Dad their newest global superstar. And fortunately, Dad was making Jake's job pretty easy.

First to suffer the Demolition Man's wrath was Simon Stoat.

There have been some legendary wrestlers to use animals as props – Bo the Constrictor terrorised the *WOW!* ring for years with Crusher, his thirty-foot pet python while Lord of the Jungle once turned up to a press conference with a leopard on a lead. (It had been a short-lived interview, as the chain snapped in two, leaving the leopard with an extensive menu laid out in front of him.)

Simon, however (by day, a health and safety officer for the council,) was allergic to cats, and chose to petrify his opponents with a stoat he'd hand-reared from birth. OK, so stoats *do* have sharp teeth, but Simon's pet, Martyn, was a vegetarian. Which meant that instead of viciously biting an opponent's thigh after being shoved down his tights, Martyn would wriggle about as if he was trying to find a rogue cashew nut tucked away in the darkness. Not exactly torture, is it? Who ever heard of a wrestler being tickled into submission?

Anyway, I digress.

Neither Simon nor Martyn were a match for the Demolition Man. Within seconds, Dad had thrust the stoat down Simon's own tights and Martyn had taken a terrified chomp out of his master's inner thigh.

After that, it was carnage. Suplexes, clotheslines, body splashes from the top rope. There wasn't a single move George didn't pull, until finally, he dispatched both stoat and wrestler over the top rope, care of the Wrecking Ball.

Jake captured every glorious second of it, just as he did when Dad beat Arthur the Fighting Farmer by chasing him around the ring with his own pitchfork. By the time the fight was over, Arthur couldn't sit down without the help of a rubber ring and a puncture repair kit.

And by the time George had dealt with the Manic Milkman, covering his bruised body in a sticky pool of rhubarb yoghurt and double cream, Jake knew he had everything he needed.

Two weeks and three days later, with the competition about to close, Floss held the world premiere of *Demolition Man – The Movie* in her front room.

Jake and Mouse settled down excitedly with huge buckets of popcorn and a vat of Coke.

'OK, you have to remember what I had to work with,' said Floss. 'The camera work is wobbly and the lighting is iffy, but—'

'You'd better be able to see the costume properly,' interrupted Mouse.

'BUT!' bellowed Floss. (This was her moment, not Mouse's.) 'I think you'll find we have achieved the desired effect. So, without further ado, laydeez and gentlemen, I give you THE DEMOLITIOOON MAAAAAN!'

The. Film. Was. Magnificent.

It was everything Jake had hoped for and more. There was drama, there was intrigue, there were moments of horror that made the Tsunami Terror look like Snow White. Or maybe the seven dwarfs.

Dopey.

Especially Dopey.

It took every bit of self-restraint Jake had to stop himself from bouncing on the settee. And by the time the credits rolled he was biting his lip with emotion.

'Awesome,' he gabbled. 'Both of you are awesome.'

Floss and Mouse tried to look cool about it all, though their grins said otherwise. They may not have thought much of wrestling, but they were buzzing to see their pal so excited.

'Should we show it to your dad, then?' said Mouse.

'Yeah, no need to keep it secret. He'll love it,' added Floss.

Jake, however, feared a different response.

There was no way he could show Dad. Dad would *eat* the film before he let Jake send it to *WOW!* Despite Floss's fancy editing, it was clearly Dad up there on the screen. All twenty-odd wobbling stone of him.

Nope, they would have to stay undercover that little bit longer. Until Arnie McBride was camped on their doorstep *begging* Dad to sign up.

Because once Dad had superstardom laid out in front of him, Jake was sure there was no way he would turn it down.

9
The House That Was Stolen

The next six weeks, four days, seventeen hours and thirty-one minutes were agony.

Imagine if you had to spend all that time lying in a dentist's chair while someone prodded your gums with a splintered lolly stick. Imagine not being allowed any painkillers either, while being forced to wear your granny's favourite nightie. THAT is a tiny fraction of how much the waiting hurt poor Jake. Each morning, he hoped to find a letter on the mat, or a voicemail on his mobile, but each morning there was nothing.

Nada.

Zilch.

It wasn't easy. Even Saturdays lost a tiny bit of their shine. What was the point of Dad taking on all-comers, when there were no decent all-comers left to come on? Dad deserved his shot at the big time, he really did, and it terrified Jake that he might miss out. What if Arnie McBride gave Dad's slot to some other bozo?

Jake tried to keep busy, but it felt as if someone had pressed his own personal pause button. He saw Floss jump into another movie project, watched enviously as Mouse drew a comic book of his own. He even felt a little jealous when he saw Masher Milner go about his bullying with a smile. Mind you, that didn't last long – not when Masher turned his attention back to Jake.

'No flab . . . I mean Dad, today?' he asked, as he and his muppets tailed Jake into school one Monday morning.

Jake tried to ignore him.

'I said – where's your old man?' The bully slapped a shocked expression on his face. 'Oh no, don't tell me it finally happened . . .?'

'What?' asked Jake.

'He hasn't finally burst, has he? I mean, it's been on the cards for years. What was it that sent him over the edge? Kebab or pizza? Don't tell me. I can guess . . . BOTH!'

His pack of hyenas howled their approval.

Jake's fuse burned perilously short, but he refused to blow. (He liked his face the way it looked.) Instead he clung on to the hope that once Dad was famous, none of this would matter any more.

The kids who lived on Storey Street had a favourite place to meet.

To anyone who didn't live there, it just looked like a scrap of wasteland. To the residents of Storey Street, it was known as The House That Was Stolen.

The House That Was Stolen – or THTWS (catchy, eh?) – was a small patch of empty-ish land that sat between two terraced houses, one of which unfortunately belonged to Masher Milner and his family. It was the only space of its kind on the whole street and was exactly house-sized and –shaped. It looked as if someone had held a huge vacuum cleaner over the top of it, and sucked a house clean away.

What made it even freakier, was that one night, long ago, someone (no one knew who) had arranged a settee, lamp and TV set in the gap where the living room would've been. The settee was old and scuzzy, and the TV didn't have a plug, but it didn't matter. The stuff looked as if it belonged there, to Storey Street's kids at least.

Some of the more miserly adults called the council and demanded the stuff be taken away, but every time the bin men cleared it, by some miraculous miracle, more stuff appeared.

A settee. A lamp. And a TV.

I know what you're thinking. But it wasn't me. Honest.

In the end, after months of to-ing and fro-ing, the council became more cheesed off than a ball of Edam and told the busybodies of Storey Street they wouldn't be coming back. Ever

since then, the kids had used it as their own personal hang-out.

They loved it there too, taking pride to make sure any rubbish was put in the bin after they'd pretended to turn out the lamp and head for home.

Floss, Mouse and Jake sat pretending to watch TV in THTWS when everything turned on its head.

Floss was enjoying *E.T. the Extra-terrestrial* for the fifty-seventh time, Mouse was reliving *Batman Forever* (again), and Jake was imagining with all his heart that he was watching his old man fight at Grapplemania. The image of Dad bouncing the Terror effortlessly off the ropes was like having his every dream flicker into reality.

None of them saw the HUGE STREEEEEEEETCH limo pull up down the road.

And none of them spotted the chauffeur sprint round to the back door, and open it for a grey-haired muscleman with sparkling white teeth and a deep mahogany tan. Not one of

them even noticed when that man walked with purpose straight to Jake's front door and rang the doorbell.

It wasn't until the bell buzzed for the eighth time, and the man's finger turned white, red, then blue with exertion, that Jake finally lifted his head, recognised the man, and let out the sort of scream that belonged only on Hallowe'en . . .

10

When A Plan Comes Together

'A-A-A-A-Arrn . . .' stammered Jake.

Mouse and Floss looked at one another, then at Jake, then back at the busted TV. He'd been acting weird ever since they'd sent the competition entry off. They'd both been praying Jake would find out quickly, in the hope that he'd go back to normal. Well, as normal as any wrestling fan ever could be.

But right now Jake was acting far from normal. His eyes were as wide as a couple of frisbees. He pointed again and again down the street.

'A-A-A-Arnie,' he finally gasped. 'M-M-McBride. At my door.'

'What's he going on about?' Floss asked.

Mouse saw the limo and put two and two together, making a grand total of three million and twenty-nine. 'Something about a bride at his door.

There's a stretch limo there. His mum must be off on a hen night.'

To be fair to Mouse, he wasn't being totally idiotic. Limousines weren't often spotted on Storey Street, though they were more common than unicorns or talking gnomes. Usually a stretch limo meant a wedding or a hen night, with sixty-five giggling women ducking into the back of it.

But, looking closer, Mouse couldn't spot any ladies wearing L-plates. All he could actually see was his best pal, running so fast it looked as if someone had popped Martyn the Stoat down his boxer shorts.

Jake couldn't believe what he was seeing. Was that really Arnie McBride? On his street? Knocking on his door? It could only mean one thing. And it wasn't as if Arnie would be wanting to borrow their vacuum cleaner.

Dad had won – they'd done it! Jake's head spun with glorious images. Flashbulbs from cameras, red carpets, Dad signing autograph after autograph. He'd be the proudest son on the face of the planet!

The only problem was, neither Mum nor Dad would have a clue what Arnie was going on about. Jake had to lay the groundwork quicker than his old dad normally knocked it down.

Unfortunately, by the time Jake reached his gate, the front door was open, and there was Mum, with Lewis hanging off her waist.

Arnie was smaller in the flesh, but no less impressive. Jake wanted to pinch him, check he was real, but was too in awe. It was really him!

'You must be Mrs Demolition!' Arnie was singing.

'Congratulations! Let me tell you, your man is a dark dark dawg! He's our winner, I tell ya, our newest *WOW!* superstar!'

Mum was squinting at a business card in her hand. Instead of looking pleased at having the word WINNER shouted in her face, she looked as if she was ready to trap Arnie's nose in the door.

'Listen, Mr McBride . . .'

'Please, call me Arnie,' Arnie schmoozed. 'All the ladies do . . .'

'Listen, *MR* McBride,' she hissed. 'I don't know what you're after, or who's told you I'm a pushover. But you'll get nowhere soft-soaping me. Go try it on with Mrs Willison at number sixty-four – she'll buy anything, that one. If you'll excuse me, I've a drain I'd rather be unblocking than speaking to you.'

As the door started to swing shut, Jake saw his hopes and dreams about to follow Mum's plunger straight down the drain. With one huge effort, he threw himself between Arnie and the door.

'Wait,' he yelled. 'It's all right, Mum. Mr McBride's not selling anything. He's here because I asked him to come. He's here to change everything. Isn't that right, Mr McBride?'

Arnie grinned at Jake, fingers curled into a gun shape. 'BOOM!' he yelled. 'I can see who has the brains around here and who has the beauty.'

'Oh, Mum's the brains *and* the beauty,' said Jake. He had no idea how he was going to explain all this to her. He'd always imagined he'd be allowed to break the news to Dad first, so hoped a bit of crawling might put her in the right mood. 'But it was me who entered Dad in the competition.' Jake paused, a flash of doubt zapping into his brain. 'You are . . . here about the competition, aren't you? It is . . . *good* news, isn't it?'

'Good news?' boomed Arnie. 'It's the best news, my boy. The BEST! Your pop's a winner. Your pop's going global, I tell you, global!'

At that moment, Jake wanted to hug Mr McBride. Heck, he felt so powerful, he thought he could lift all eighteen stone of him and swing him round by the ears. Unfortunately, as awesome as that image is (and what a brilliant illustration it would make . . . *Look! Look below!*), it didn't quite happen.

'Competition?' Mum asked irritably. 'What competition? Not the one on the back of the Choco Pops box? Jake, I've told you before, we don't want a lifetime's supply of chocolate cereal. Your dad's fat enough as it is.'

Arnie laughed. 'Chocolate cereal? Are you kidding me? Ma'am, ain't no way you and your family are eating chocolate cereal ever again. From this point on, it's smoked salmon and caviar, it's roast pheasant and champagne, baby!!'

Mum looked so confused now that her head was in danger of exploding. However, as the neighbours had started to gather around Arnie's luxury limo, she decided to carry on in private. 'Why don't you come inside, Mr McBride? Just for a minute, mind. Just so you can explain exactly what it is we've won.'

Arnie didn't need to be asked twice. He squeezed his bulk through the doorframe and into the living room. Jake bounded after him.

'So,' said Mum, half intrigued, half sceptical. 'Tell us about this competition of yours.'

Jake was still panicking. He knew that Arnie only had to say the word 'wrestling' and Mum would boot him right back out of the door. He had to find an angle that would sell it to her. And he had to find it quickly.

He looked at Mum, then spotted her travel magazines lying on the coffee table, and *WHAM!* Salvation hit him like a jumbo jet, straight between the eyes.

'Tell her about all the travel, Mr McBride,' stammered Jake, hoping the American would see his panic and help him out.

Arnie looked at Jake, then at Mum, then back at Jake. Sheesh, he'd been warned Brits were eccentric, but this lot were whack-jobs!

'Shouldn't we wait for your dad first? Give *him* the good news?'

Mum's foot was beginning to tap impatiently. She always did that when her temper was fraying. Jake turned to Arnie, his eyes pleading.

'The travel?' said Arnie, thankfully taking the hint. 'You mean the first class, unlimited air travel to the greatest cities on earth?'

Mum's eyes widened.

Arnie could see he'd hit a sweet spot.

'Not to mention the six-star hotels in LA, Vegas, Sydney and Hong Kong.'

'Six-star? I didn't know there was such a thing,' said Mum. Jake thought he could almost see the palm trees and beaches reflected in her eyes.

'For you, my darlin,' Arnie crooned. 'I'd open a string of them.'

Mum's expression changed then. All the wrinkles and worry seemed to fall away and she looked as happy as a mouse who'd inherited a cheese factory.

Jake sagged in relief onto the arm of the chair, before the front door opened and Dad ambled in.

'There's a limo outside, Luce,' he said. 'You off on a hen d—'

But he didn't finish his sentence as his eyes landed on Arnie.

Now George was a good man, a warm man. He loved his wife and kids as much as he loved eating a rack of ribs as big as a T-rex. But he'd never dreamed that he'd come home from work to find one of his heroes, a man whose wrestling show he'd watched every week for years, standing in HIS front room. And when it happened? Well, he didn't know what to make of it. He wondered if the three-foot prawn baguette he'd scoffed on the way home had given him some weird food poisoning that had addled his brain.

'George Biggs,' Arnie said, his arms open wide. 'Georgey B, my main man. I'm here to change your life! I'm here to make you rich! You're going to be more famous than the freaking Queen!'

There was a moment of silence as a new world dawned in the Biggs household. Dad's eyes bulged. Mum's mouth hung open. Lewis announced he needed a wee. And as for Jake? Jake smiled. Grapplemania had just edged a whole lot closer.

The Reluctant Hero

George Biggs was confused. It felt like his brain was being used as a dishrag. If he wasn't mistaken, here, in front of him, was a legend. A bona fide superstar. In his living room. He had a million questions, but couldn't ask any of them because it felt as if someone had replaced his tongue with a piece of sandpaper.

Jake wondered if he should wave some food in front of Dad's face – anything to snap him out of his daze. He couldn't let Arnie get fed up and walk out!

'Low blood sugar,' Jake said, grinning at their American guest. 'He's just the same before a big fight.'

Arnie nodded; he wasn't sure what else he could do.

'Dad,' Jake said. 'Mum, don't look so confused. Mr McBride's here with knockout news!'

'You betcha cute boots it's knockout!' said Arnie.

'You see,' interrupted Jake, desperate to stay in control, 'I entered Dad in this competition.' He paused. He knew he needed to make it sound good – so good that neither of them could possibly say no.

'Dad, you're the best, you know that. The best demolisher, the best dad and the BEST wrestler.' George smiled at the compliment, despite feeling uneasy and confused. He wanted to ask what exactly was going on, though Jake wouldn't give him the chance. Not yet. 'And Mum, well, you're the best at everything else. But it can't be easy being stuck here looking after Lewis and me. Not after being such a jetsetter.'

Mum blushed.

'So I thought, if I entered Dad in this competition, we'd finally get the chance to show everyone what an amazing wrestler he is, and Mum, you'd get to travel again . . .'

Dad was frowning. 'It's not as easy as that, Jake. And besides, you know the rules about wrestling. It's a hobby and nothing else! Plus, I can't just go swanning off. I've got responsibilities. I've got a job.'

'A job?' said Arnie, laughing. 'Why would you need a job when you can be a SUPERSTAR? A two-hundred-carat-gold *WOW!* legend. You're my winner, George. Over a million people entered, but I want YOU to fight and BEAT the Terror at Grapplemania. Then I'm taking you all over the world. Heck, by the time I'm finished with you, you'll be fighting on the moon!'

Mum looked ready to faint. The moon? How many stars did the hotels have in outer space?

Jake didn't say anything. This was even better than he'd expected! He watched Dad look over at Mum, a serious expression on both of their faces. Then slowly, Dad crossed the room towards Arnie and stretched out his hand.

This was WAY easier than Jake had thought it would be.

'Mr McBride,' Dad said. 'You are a legend in our house. Jake and me have been watching you for years. I'm not lying when I say that this is an amazing opportunity, or when I tell you we are

WOW!'s number one fans—'

Jake couldn't believe it. He felt like jumping for joy. Dad was saying ALL the right things in exactly the right order.

'—which makes it doubly difficult for me to say thank you, sir. But no, thanks. I, well . . . we . . . we can't accept your kind offer.'

Hang on. Was Dad joking? Arnie had already said they'd had over a million entries. This wasn't the time to mess around.

'But Dad. Mr McBride's come all the way from America – in a limo . . .' Jake stuttered.

'And I'm sorry if it's been a wasted trip,' said Dad. 'But I didn't ask him to come.'

Arnie was the one who was confused now. He pulled a piece of neatly folded paper from his pocket.

'Of course you asked me to come. I've got your signature right here.'

Dad squinted at the paper being shoved under his nose.

'It's my signature,' he sighed, and turned to Jake with a suspicious frown. 'But I didn't write it.'

Jake shifted from foot to foot. 'Er, actually, you did, Dad. I told you it was a permission form for a school trip.'

'Jake!' yelled Mum and Dad in unison.

'But I did it for the right reasons,' Jake insisted. 'Because I wanted everyone to know how good you are.' It was just SO FRUSTRATING! If Jake was as good as Dad at something, there was NO WAY he'd be so shy about it.

'Good?!' yelled Arnie. 'GOOD?! With our help, you'll be better than good. You'll be famous. There'll be mugs, caps, posters and T-shirts, all with your face on them. I'm going to put you on the television in every country in the world. There ain't a billboard big enough to hold what you got!'

'I didn't start fighting so I could be on billboards,' Dad said, frowning. 'It was something just for me and Jake. It was meant to be a secret!'

'Some secrets, my friend,' said Arnie, 'are too big to keep. Sometimes . . .' He looked dramatically into mid-air, with a sideways glance at Mum. 'Sometimes you have to share the secret with America and Australia and Hong Kong and Russia.'

'Well,' said Dad. 'I'm afraid this is one secret that won't even make it past the front door. I'm sorry, Mr McBride. We didn't mean to waste your time.'

Jake felt his world collapse. It wasn't supposed to be like this. It was supposed to be the best moment in the history of the world. And Dad was throwing it all away. It felt like the Terror had dropped every ounce of his gut on top of him, leaving him breathless and panicky. How much trouble was he going to be in when Arnie left? The disappointment and worry was suddenly all too much, and Jake felt tears prickling behind his eyes.

Now, Jake wasn't really a crier, so when he buried his head in his hands, Dad sank to his knees beside him.

'Jake?' Dad said gently. 'Come on, son. It's a competition, that's all.'

'No, it's not, it's more than that,' Jake wept, tears falling freely now. He didn't care who saw; he'd never wanted something as much as he wanted this. 'It's much more important than that.'

'Well, then you should have talked to me and your mum about it. You should have told us what you were doing.'

'What? So you could say no then, instead of now?'

'At least then you wouldn't have gone to all this effort.
Wouldn't have got your hopes so high.'

'I only got my hopes high because it matters. Because this
could be our chance, Dad – our chance to change everything.
To make everything brilliant.'

Dad was confused. 'But why do we need to change anything?
Saturdays are already brilliant.'

Jake looked Dad in the eye.

'They are, but I'm tired of seeing you wrestle in front of a
bunch of grannies, of fighting people who aren't fit to tie your
boots. You deserve more than that. You should be loved by

millions.' Jake felt the pride ripple through his body. 'People should cheer when they see you on the telly or on the side of a cereal box. I don't care if it's Russia or Mongolia, or even on Mars, – everyone should know who the Demolition Man is. Because then, just maybe, Masher Milner wouldn't be able to say you're a useless lump of lard . . .'

Jake gasped and threw his hands to his mouth. He didn't know how that last bit had slipped out.

Dad's eyes flared. So did his nostrils.

'Is that what he calls me?'

Jake shrugged. He hated how it sounded out loud, but he couldn't take the words back.

'Sometimes. Sometimes he calls you Jabba, or Gutlord, or Wobblebott—'

'I get the message,' Dad said, sighing. 'And does this bother you?'

'Course it does. I hate it. Cos I know how amazing you are at wrestling, and if he saw you, just once, he'd know too, and so would everyone else.'

George rubbed his face, weighing everything up.

The prospect of the world seeing him wobble in his skin-tight costume, his wife's inevitable embarrassment, the possibility of being squashed flat by the Tsunami. But then he looked at Jake and remembered each and every Saturday they'd spent together, the pride they felt at what they'd achieved. And as for all this? Well, he could see clearly what it meant to Jake.

Maybe some things *were* too big to keep secret? Maybe he owed it to Jake to make him happy?

Hauling himself off his knees, he turned back to Arnie.

'Where do I sign?' he asked.

'You already did!' said the American, pointing at Jake's signature. 'Welcome to the world of *WOW!*'

12

Seacross's Favourite Son . . .

Seacross had never seen the likes of it.

You see, no one ever really visited the town any more. There was no need, thanks to cheap holidays in the sun. Plus, there was no road through Seacross. Anyone daft enough to keep on driving ended up with a soggy gearbox as they crashed over the cliffs into the North Sea.

But today, all that had changed. The roads teemed with traffic, the pavements bulged with pedestrians, TV vans filled every car park, and there were helicopters circling in the sky.

The craziest bit, though, was that no one knew exactly what they were excited about – not even the local TV channel that had broken the news the night before, after a secretive message from the world-famous Arnie McBride. The reporter had interrupted their headline piece about a missing wheeliebin. Nobody seemed to mind.

'This bombshell just in . . .' faltered Kyle Ramsbottom, the anchorman. 'Tomorrow morning, at ten o'clock, *World of Wrestling*'s Arnie McBride will hold a press conference at City Hall. News crews from all over the globe are descending on our little town, to witness what has been described as an "earth–

shattering announcement".'

The rumours spread as if someone had set fire to wildfire.

The Queen would be donning a leotard and fighting under the name 'The Monarch of Madness'.

But then why announce it in Seacross?

Was she moving Buckingham Palace up there brick by brick?

Would the rest of the south of England relocate too?

It didn't make a jot of sense, but that just made everyone even more excited, even the people who'd never watched wrestling in their life.

Twenty-four hours after Arnie's arrival, City Hall was fizzing like a can of pop inside a washing machine being driven at a hundred miles an hour down a cobbled street.

People squeezed into every seat, aisle and cranny they could find.

Arnie McBride was in his element, his tan so shiny he looked as if he'd been polished with a duster. As he walked onto the stage with a single spotlight following him, the *WOW!* theme tune belted out of the speakers. He reached centrestage and a cluster of fireworks erupted around him, much to the delight of the crowd.

In the wings, beside Dad, Jake was a whirlwind of excitement. He didn't spot the gaggle of grannies from Dad's last fight, practically drooling with excitement. All he could see was a sea of mobile phones held aloft, and a blizzard of flashes as Arnie waved and beamed. It was brilliant that everyone seemed to love *WOW!* just as much as he did!

'SEACROSS, ENGLAAAAND!' Arnie yelled into a microphone taped to his cheek. 'ENGLAAAAAND, SEACROOOSS!'

Some of the crowd raised an eyebrow, wondering if this man really knew where he was.

'I am over the freakin' moon to see you guys filling this place. For months now, I've been scouring the planet for a new superstar to take on the heavyweight champion of the world, the most fearsome wrestler this planet has ever seen – the Tsunami Terror.'

The non-wrestling fans looked bemused, as if Arnie was talking a strange, ancient language, before a life-sized hologram of the Terror appeared at his side. With a roar of 'Seacross is for LOSERS,' the hologram threw his arms out towards the audience. So life-like and terrifying was it that a kid on the front row farted. Then ran for the loo.

The crowd, insulted, booed the hologram. How dare he insult their town?

Arnie milked it like the legend he was. 'You see, the Tsunami Terror doesn't like this country of yours. In fact, he hates this town in particular. Because what he's found out – and what you don't know yet – is that the greatest undiscovered wrestler of our time, the biggest threat to his unbeaten record, has been living among you, right here in Seacliff . . .'

'SEACROSS!' yelled someone from the back.

'Exactly,' said Arnie. 'Can you believe it? He's walked among you all his life. The man who is going to end the reign of terror. The man who is going to pull the plug on the Tidal Wave. Right here in Soulcross.'

The person shouted again, but was drowned out by surprised gasps from the crowd. Could it be true? People whispered and looked around them, trying to guess who it might possibly be.

The little kid walking back from the toilet heard the news, farted and ran for the loo again.

'Oh, you won't find him out there,' said Arnie. 'Cos I got him up here, backstage. So tell me, are you ready to meet him?'

The crowd were on their feet now, united in one word. 'YES!'

'I can't hear you, people. Don't you want to meet your hero? The man who is going to make your town and YOU just as famous as he will be? Heck, he'll be so famous I'll build a theme park right here! Wanna meet him?'

'YEEESSS!' they yelled again.

'Well, here he is. The man who's going to put the soul back into Soulcross, the man who will have tourists flocking here, filling your pockets and your bellies . . . MR GEORGEY BEEEEEEE!'

Jake held his breath. This was it. What would people do when they saw Dad? Would they still be excited or would they just laugh?

He looked up at Dad, who was standing beside him, focused and steely. Jake had seen that expression many times. His fight face. He couldn't wait for Seacross to find out just how cool and tough and *amazing* his old man was.

Then, before he had a chance to think about it any further, Dad took a deep breath and strode out onto the stage.

Jake needn't have worried about the crowd though, because it was clear that Arnie McBride was a maestro who could sell a rhubarb salad to a ravenous lion. And the people of Seacross, at that moment in time, could think of nothing except how yumpcious rhubarb was.

All right, so there were a few baffled faces from those who knew George, like his workmates, but by now the atmosphere in the room was so intense that they had no choice but to believe that George Biggs, with his huge gut, bald head and bushy beard, was everything Arnie said he was: the next Wrestling Champion of the World.

Cheers filled the air. Cheers, whoops and screams. There wasn't a single laugh or titter. Applause bounced around the room.

Even the farty kid, back from the loos, controlled his gut enough to shout his approval.

Dad had never experienced anything like it. He smiled and waved at the crowd like it was the most natural thing in the world. Jake felt like he was having an out-of-body experience. He didn't think he'd ever known happiness like it.

Arnie beckoned Jake on from the wings.

'And now let me introduce you to the little guy who made this all possible,' Arnie said, as Jake joined him and Dad in the spotlight. 'It was Jake, here, who entered George in the competition. Both of these guys are champions!'

Arnie stood between Dad and Jake, holding their arms aloft. Jake whooped in delight. There wasn't a word in the dictionary that could sum up how amazing he felt.

He spotted Mouse and Floss, standing on chairs and cheering; he even thought he saw Masher Milner, wearing a huge foam finger and waving it joyously in their direction.

The cheering and the flashing cameras seemed to go on forever. Finally Arnie took questions from the journalists waving their microphones at the front of the stage.

'What will this mean in reality for Seacross?'

'Is it true you're going to build a theme park here?'

'And hotels?'

'And you're offering new jobs for everyone who wants one?'

The crowd got more and more excited with every nod from Arnie McBride. So did Jake. All these wonderful things were going to happen, thanks to him and Dad. He could hardly believe it.

The questions continued.

'How long have you been fighting, George?'

'What's your record?'

'How do you train your dad for a big bout?'

Arnie had spent the night before telling Dad and Jake what to say. They managed their answers perfectly, until Arnie shouted, 'One last question!'

'What's George's wrestling name?' yelled a reporter from the *Seacross Gazette*.

'Yeah,' boomed another from *Grappling Monthly*. 'Is he the Seacross Psycho?'

'Or the Fat Phantom?'

'How about the Northern Nutter?' yelled another.

Jake shook his head and prepared to shout the truth. It was the moment he'd looked forward to most. The moment they would announce the Demolition Man to the world.

But Arnie got there first.

'There'll be opportunities to talk about that later, fellas. For now, all you need to know is that by the time old Arnie McBride has finished with Georgey B, he'll be even more fearsome than he already is. Now, if you'll excuse us, we've a jet to catch.'

The words splintered inside Jake's head. He knew Dad was leaving tonight for an intensive training camp. And that he was leaving without him. It still didn't seem fair. So what if he missed a few weeks of school?

Mum had thought otherwise.

'No way,' she'd said, folding her arms. 'You've never missed school for wrestling, and that's not about to start now.'

'But, Mu-um, it'll soon be the end of term . . .' Jake whined.

'That doesn't change a thing . . .'

'Dad needs me,' he tried.

'Jake,' said Mum. 'It will be a cold day in hell when wrestling comes before school.'

He'd begged Mum to change her mind, but when she'd threatened to ban him from the big night itself, he finally took a reluctant vow of silence.

Now, Jake smiled proudly as Dad slid off the front of the stage to shake people's hands. Scraps of paper were thrust into his hands to sign. Everyone wanted a bit of him.

'There'll be time for autographs when we bring the championship belt home,' boomed Arnie, shepherding Dad through the crowd towards the limo waiting out front.

The only problem was, the crowd were so excited they wouldn't let Dad through.

'Come on, people. Let the big man pass!' Arnie shouted.

But the crowd wasn't prepared to see their man simply walk out of there. Oh no. They were going to give him a send-off fit for a star.

'Georgey B's Seacross Army!' they chanted, and as their song rose to a crescendo, a handful of Dad's burly workmates hoisted him above their heads. With an ease that made it look like he weighed a weedy fifty kilograms, they crowd-surfed him across the hall.

Imagine that! A man the size of a barn gliding effortlessly

through the air, cos that's exactly what happened.

He was like a rock star! Jake thought, his heart swelling with pride. He scrambled back onto the stage, pulling Mouse and Floss up with him.

Floss reached for her camera, but Jake stopped her. He didn't need her to film it. He was recording every second in his brain, where no one had access it to it except him. Somewhere nobody could ever delete it.

Finally, Dad was carried through the front doors and out to the limo, his feet never once touching the ground.

And that was it. He was gone.

Well, nearly.

Outside, the crowd surrounded Arnie's limo. The street resembled a train carriage in rush hour, and for a second Jake thought they might lift the limo and carry it to the airport. But gradually, and with the singing only getting louder, the limo edged gently away.

'Go get him,' Jake whispered as Dad met his eye with a wink. 'Make me proud.'

How could he possibly do anything else?

13

Living the Dream

Jake Biggs was living the dream.

Dad was going to be a *World of Wrestling!* superstar, simple as that.

He'd always known winning the competition would make Dad the most famous person in Seacross's history, but he hadn't understood what that would actually mean. Not really.

Now though, a week after the big announcement, Dad had become the centre of *everyone's* world, instead of just Jake's. His face filled every TV screen and newspaper, not just the day after the news broke, but every day since.

Local radio shows were just as obsessed: there were phone-ins to discuss what Dad's success would mean for the town, debates about his chances of pinning the Tsunami Terror. Suddenly there were hundreds of stories about Dad. An elderly man called Mr Murray phoned Seacross FM radio and said he was Dad's old headmaster. He claimed to be responsible for Dad's toughness, having caned him every day for years. A lady called Lola kept ringing in too, saying she was Dad's first girlfriend. Mum turned scarlet whenever her voice came on, and turned the radio off before banging every pot or pan in the kitchen.

Adults, Jake thought, were just plain weird.

Put simply, the people of Seacross were besotted with George Biggs, and united in their determination to see him victorious. Because if he won? Well, it would feel as if the whole town had won too. Arnie would build his wrestling theme park. And with the theme park would come tourists, and tourists meant new hotels and restaurants and jobs. Arnie and Dad were going to drag Seacross into the twenty-first century.

Jake felt like he was floating on a sea of arms just like Dad at City Hall. It had been Dad's skills that made all this possible, but Jake knew he'd done his bit too. Arnie had said so, and that made him proud every second of the day.

There had been a wonderful moment at school when the kids in his class had swept him off his feet and paraded him round the playground.

Even Masher Milner was giving him a wide berth these days.

Can you believe it? Jake couldn't.

When they passed on the street now, the meathead didn't terrorise Jake. Instead he'd nod in his direction before locking horns with some other poor unsuspecting soul.

Jake felt guilty that someone else was getting the flak, but he was relieved too.

'Doesn't take brain surgery to work out why he's leaving you alone,' Mouse said.

'No, course not,' Jake replied, though he didn't *really* understand. 'Er…why?'

'Think about it. If your dad makes Seacross famous, like Arnie says he will, it's Masher's dad who'll make the most money.'

'What do you mean?' said Jake.

'Think about it: Maurice Milner owns Milner, Milner and Milner, the estate agent's. He's sold just about every building in Seacross.'

It was true – you never saw a 'For Sale' sign without Maurice's ugly mug beaming down at you.

'So all of Arnie's plans will mean mega-sales and mega-dosh for the Milners. Have you not heard Masher bragging about it?' Mouse imitated the bully's hulking frame and gruff voice. *'First thing we're going to do is buy a fleet of cars. Rolls-Royces and Porsches. Then we'll get a new house with a pool and a tennis court. Then Dad says I can get gold teeth. And maybe diamond fillings.'*

Jake shuddered. Masher was unbearable enough now; what would he be like if he suddenly had all this money and a gob full of bling?

He chose not to think about it, and tried to focus on imagining the moment Dad would drive the Terror into the canvas with his mighty Wrecking Ball. It was weird, though, seeing Dad everywhere he went, especially when he was on the other side of the Atlantic. The house felt much bigger without him. The kitchen cupboards were a lot fuller too, though Jake couldn't

bring himself to eat the chocolate cereal, saving it up for Dad's victorious return.

With weeks to wait until he, Mum and Lewis were due to fly out to Vegas for the big fight, Jake perked himself up with regular Skype calls, speaking to Dad as he reclined in a hotel room that looked as big as Jake's school. He peppered Dad with question after question.

'Which wrestlers have you met? Have you learned any new moves? Do they have Choco Pops in America?'

All too often the calls were brief.

'Got to train,' Dad would say, or, 'Off to do an interview.'

Jake always ended their chats trying to sound cheerful, when he felt anything but. He'd have given anything to be there alongside Dad.

After the first week, technology started to betray them. Every time the family called, there was no reply. Jake started to worry. How would he be able to tell if Dad was training too hard or not eating enough if he couldn't even talk to him?

Nine days and dozens of failed attempts later, Jake decided to phone the hotel and, after speaking to three different receptionists (none of whom could understand a word he said), finally got through to Dad's room.

A voice that Jake didn't recognise answered. It was reedy and thin, the voice of someone who only had the strength to sharpen pencils for a living.

'Hello, can I speak to George, please?' Jake asked.

'Jake?' said the voice.

'Er . . . yes. Who's that?'

'It's Dad!'

Jake wondered if he'd got the times wrong. Why did Dad sound so strange?

'Did I wake you up?'

'No,' Dad said defensively, though he *was* prone to a snooze after one of his gargantuan afternoon snacks.

'We've been trying to Skype you for days,' Jake said.

There was a pause. 'Have you? Oh . . . there's been a problem with the broadband, actually . . . it keeps breaking.'

Jake frowned. Hang on. This was America. Wasn't everything supposed to be bigger and better over there? Hot dogs the size of canoes, burgers the size of cars – surely their broadband should be wider than a motorway?

'I tried your mobile too.'

'Must be out of battery.'

'No, no it's not,' Jake frowned. None of this was adding up. 'It rang 'til your voicemail kicked in. Dad, is everything OK?'

'OK? Yeah, course it is. Don't I sound OK?'

Jake fought the temptation to tell the truth. He wanted to say Dad sounded ill, or tired, or kind of sad. 'You sound . . . different.'

'Oh, that's just jetlag.'

'But you've been there over a week.'

'Yeah but . . . I was sitting at the back of the plane. It takes longer to wear off.'

'Wow,' said Jake. He had no idea that happened. He'd never been on a ferry, never mind an aeroplane.

'How's the training going?'

'Training?' Dad's voice got higher. Jake hoped it was with enthusiasm. 'It's full-on. They're finding muscles in places where I didn't even think I had flab.'

'But you are still eating, aren't you? We don't want you losing too much weight. It's not good for you!'

'Oh, don't you worry. There are people here watching everything very carefully.'

'Good.' Dad sounded more like himself now and Jake felt a bit better. 'What about your costume? They're not changing it too much, are they? 'Cos we agreed that we—'

'Can we talk about something else?' Dad asked suddenly. 'I'm sorry, Jake. It's just, I'm either talking wrestling, or practising it every minute of the day. And, well, I miss you lot. Go on, tell me about something else.'

Something else? What else *was* there? Him and Dad didn't do *anything else*. Wrestling was their thing.

What followed was ten minutes of awkward conversation about the weather and school. You know, the stuff no one *really* wants to talk about.

By the time Jake put down the phone, he felt a twinge of fear in his stomach. It nibbled away so hungrily that he could think of nothing else.

Something was going on. Dad *loved* talking about wrestling. If he didn't want to speak to Jake about it, he must have found someone to take his place. A new trainer, someone with more experience, an ex-fighter maybe? Maybe even Arnie himself? A painful thought crashed into Jake's head. That was it. Jake was being sacked!

Well, he wasn't having it. Not after everything he'd done: the costume, the name, the signature move. They couldn't forget about him after all that!

Jake ran to the kitchen and grabbed Arnie McBride's business card from the notice board. Without hesitation he hammered the mobile number into the phone and waited for the great man to pick up.

'YO YO YO!' Arnie cried. It sounded as though he was standing in the middle of a nightclub. 'Speak to me!'

'Hello, Arnie, it's Jake Biggs. From Seacross.'

'Jim from Slowcliff? I don't know no Jim from Slowcliff. Wrong number, dude—'

'Not Slowcliff, SEACROSS! It's Jake, George Biggs's son.'

There was a pause. He could almost hear the cogs in Arnie's brain turning.

'Jakey, my boy! My main man! How's it goin'?'

'Er, it's going well, thanks, Mr McBride. Or it was, until I spoke to my dad. He's not his normal self today.'

Arnie laughed. It sounded like a machine gun.

'Course he's not his normal self, son, his life's about to change forever! In two weeks' time he steps into the ring with an irresistible force, an immovable object. And if he beats him, he'll be more famous than the President of the US of A.'

'I get that, Mr McBride, but Dad won't talk to me about it. And that's dangerous, 'cos he's never prepared for a fight without me there. I'm his trainer.'

'And a great job you've done, too, my boy. But you have to trust Uncle Arnie now. I've been promoting wrestlers since you were a glint in your daddy's eye.'

'But he's cutting me out of things, like he doesn't need my advice.'

There was another pause.

'Your daddy loves you, son, you know that?'

Jake nodded, forgetting he was on the phone.

'And he wants to do what's best. For you, for your momma and your brother and for all those people in Sealcroft who are relying on him.'

'I know that already . . .'

'So he needs to focus on the Terror. If he goes into that ring and gets squashed just like all those other bums before him? Well, the dream ends there and then. For you, for him, for everyone in your town.'

Jake felt faint. 'What are you trying to say?'

'I didn't want to tell you like this, Jake, but now that you're on the phone . . . well, your daddy and me, we think you and your momma and brother should watch this one from home. Let Georgey take down the Terror without any distractions – after that you can be ringside every time. You understand what I'm saying to you, boy?'

Jake couldn't say anything. His mum always told him not to swear, though when she found out the news she'd be inventing some new rude words herself.

'It's for the best. Just this one time. Your daddy wanted to tell you himself, but he couldn't do it to ya. That's why old Arnie is, to save him the heartache.'

Heartache. Jake had never really known what that meant until now. Until Arnie had popped the bubble he'd been living in. Now he felt it in every muscle of his body. Total and utter devastation.

Las Vegas suddenly felt a long, long way away, and so did Dad.

14

Grapplemania!!

And so, the big day arrived, which was just as well, because:

    a) I love this bit of the story, it gets properly juicy

    b) My laptop's about to run out of battery so I need to type quickly

and

    c) Because Jake Biggs was about to go bonkers with anticipation.

This was the pot of gold at the end of the rainbow, the grand finale to everything Jake had dreamed of. Dad was fighting in Grapplemania. It was his moment to become a wrestling hero in every country of the world. Though in this dream, Jake had always been at Dad's side, his right-hand man – training him, feeding him up, ironing his leotard. He'd never expected he wouldn't be there for Dad's big fight. He certainly never thought that Dad might not need him any more.

After his conversation with Arnie, Jake hadn't called Dad. The disappointment of missing the fight made it just too hard. It was hard for all the family.

Jake texted him instead.

Good idea I miss fight. Was going to suggest to Arnie myself.

Really? Dad texted back.

Sure. Jake lied. When you're champ I won't miss a single bout. You try and stop me!

Jake pressed send, even though his heart splintered.

You're the best, son. Thanks.

Cos I take after you. Smash the Terror, Dad. Everyone here believes in you.

And it was true.

All over town there were billboards with Dad's face on. Even the Storey Street Church proudly displayed a message praying for Dad, hoping he'd flatten the Terror. 'Give him hell, George!' it read. (Jake never had the Reverend Christmas down as a grappling fan.) And apparently the council were voting on

whether to rename Storey Street 'Demolition Drive' in Dad's honour. It had a ring to it, Jake thought.

Things continued to improve at school. Teachers seemed to be marking his homework more kindly, while Masher showed even more signs of being human, when he reprimanded a kid who'd shoved Jake over in the canteen queue.

Jake thought he was living in la-la land when Masher pulled him to his feet and apologised on behalf of the kid who'd pushed him.

Everyone wanted to talk to Jake.

Is your dad confident? they'd ask.

How is he going to dispatch the Terror?

How did World War I start?

Oh, hang on, someone did ask him that, but that was Miss Doherty in History. Jake didn't have a clue, but he answered the other kids with what they wanted to hear.

'He's super-confident.'

'He's bringing the Heavyweight belt home to Seacross.'

And he believed it too, despite feeling that part of the adventure had been wrestled away from him. It all felt a bit . . . empty.

Anyway. Back to fight night.

Two thousand City Hall tickets had sold in three minutes. The fight would be beamed live from Vegas in the middle of the night (Vegas was eight hours behind Seacross) and the Biggs family were guests of honour.

On the stroke of midnight on 24 July, Jake, Mum (and a sleeping Lewis) left their house in a limo, hired by Arnie.

It was a stupid hour to be watching wrestling. Jake knew this because Mum repeated it over and over again all the way into town.

Unsurprisingly, she was still upset that her first trip had been cancelled, and she'd found it hard to talk about the fight for days without getting upset. Jake wished he could change things for her, but he was as powerless as she was.

He squeezed her hand as they sat in the limo. 'Next time it'll be different,' he said, smiling. 'Next time we'll be right there with him.'

Mum smiled and dabbed at her eyes when she thought Jake wasn't looking.

Dad's fight with the Terror was the headline act, the last one on, which would be at about five in the morning, but there was no way Jake wanted to miss a second of the coverage. Not if it meant catching an early glimpse of Dad.

The journey to City Hall was slow. The roads were packed with cars blowing their horns, and people hanging out of their sunroofs, bellowing George's name.

Grapplemania was the perfect excuse for a party, and thanks to Arnie McBride, expectations were as high as . . . well, use your imagination – mine's just run out. It's not easy, you know, coming up with witty asides all the time.

By the time Jake, Mum and Lewis arrived at the venue, the queue was snaking round the building like a snake (don't worry, my imagination *will* come back, it just takes time . . . and lots of cups of tea . . . and chocolate, if you want to send me any).

But of course the Biggs family didn't have to join the queue. The Mayor met them at their limo and led them through the crowd, who cheered and clapped as they passed.

Inside City Hall, the atmosphere was just as electric. Raucous music pumped through the speakers, people danced on chairs and shouted George's name. Taking his front row seat next to Mouse, Floss and their parents, Jake looked around in wonder.

If this was what it was like five hours before the fight, what would happen when Dad finally got into the ring?

The energy in the room was so infectious that he, Mouse, Floss, and even Mum and Lewis (who had woken up and thought he was in some kind of dreamland), joined the rest of the crowd on their chairs, singing and dancing. A constant stream of people asked Jake for photos and autographs. Jake felt as famous as his dad.

The opening fights from Vegas came and went in a blur, the greatest athletes on the planet pitting their wits and brawn against each other. The floor practically shook as one wrestler after another was slammed onto the mat.

Jake shuddered. He'd never really noticed before just how much pain the fighters were in when someone clotheslined them, or put them in a headlock, or kicked them in their nether regions. Suddenly Jake's body ached in sympathy and sweat poured from his forehead.

'One more fight to go,' barked the commentator, Tiger Fury, much to the delight of the Seacross crowd, many of whose eyes were slowly drooping after four solid hours of wrestling, 'until

our headline World Championship bout, when THE TSUNAMI TERROR takes on our newest *WOW!* superstar, George Biggs, all the way from Sawcross, England . . .'

'SEACROSS!!' yelled 1,999 voices.

How Jake wished he could be backstage with Dad, talking tactics. It was amazing seeing everyone's love for George, but a tiny part of Jake wished he didn't have to share Dad's greatest moment with so many others.

'It seems like a mismatch to the whole world,' continued Tiger. 'The most fearsome grappler on the planet versus a complete unknown. Arnie McBride has kept his newest star, George Biggs, completely under wraps. So, the question is, does he have what it takes to do what no other *WOW!* fighter has done? Can any man pin the Terror for the count of three? Folks, it won't be long until the WHOLE WORLD finds out.'

The whole world, thought Jake. That was a big place. Like a squazillion times bigger than anything he could comprehend. And if everything went to plan, soon, his dad was going to be sitting on top of it.

15

Introducing, in the Red Corner...

It was all going on in Vegas.

In the penultimate face-off, Crashmat McNasty had just thrown Smashmouth Simmons over not only the top rope, but

the first three rows of the audience as well. It wasn't the sort of landing you got up from. Smashmouth was one of the toughest wrestlers on the circuit, a man capable of reducing his opponents to quivering piles of blancmange, so when Jake saw him carted out of there on a stretcher? Well, it sent his heart thudding.

'So, folks,' roared Tiger, 'that leaves us with just one fight to go. And what a Grapplemania it's been! But hang on to your hats, because you ain't seen nothing yet!'

And with that, the hall went dark. The Seacross crowd wolf-whistled, then fell silent, as a red laser appeared on the screen, scribbling a shape that everyone strained to make out. Then there was a white laser, and a blue one too, darting from right to left in a frenzy that resulted, some thirty seconds later, in a magnificent Union Jack flag.

Jake had goosebumps on his goosebumps. This was it. The moment the Demolition Man would appear.

'And now, Grapplemaniacs,' boomed the ring announcer, 'Introducing, for the first time, all the way from the United Kingdom in England, our newest *WOW!* Suuuuuper Staaaaar . . . The BEEFEATER, Georgey BEEEEEEEEEEEEEEE!'

City Hall went inter-planetary! Hands were clapping, voices were whooping and cheering.

Jake, Mouse, Floss and Mum were confused. Mighty confused.

'What did the announcer just call him?' Mouse yelled in Jake's ear.

'*The Beefeater?*' shouted Floss in the other.

'That can't be right,' stuttered Jake. Weren't Beefeaters the guys in the funny outfits who lived at the Tower of London? Why in the name of Martyn the Stoat's droppings was the announcer calling Dad a Beefeater?

His mind raced back to Arnie's press conference. It might have been a month ago, but it was ingrained in his memory. And now that he thought about it, Arnie had *never* mentioned the name the Demolition Man. Not once. Was that because he'd planned to change it all along? And if Arnie had got rid of the name, what else had he got rid of? What about Dad's signature move, his costume, his hair—

Jake's brain didn't have time to complete that last thought, because there, on the big screen, was Dad. At least, he *thought* it was Dad. It looked like Dad.

Sort of.

Only this Dad clearly hadn't eaten in a month. This Dad didn't have a beard or ponytail. This Dad, instead of filling every inch of a custom-made Demolition-themed costume, was wearing a silly mushroom hat and a red-and-black suit that looked WAY too hot for mid-summer in Las Vegas.

This Dad was a shadow of the man who'd left Seacross just five weeks ago. He looked as if he could only manage one roast chicken instead of a dozen and . . . hang on, what was that perched on his shoulder? Jake squinted at the screen. It looked like a bird, a crow or something . . .

'It's a raven,' Floss shouted in his ear. 'There are loads of them at the Tower of London, where the Beefeaters live. They reckon if all the ravens left the Tower the whole building would collapse!'

Jake appreciated the history lesson, but he had no flipping idea what any of that had to do with his dad.

Dad didn't look happy about the bird's presence either, and nor did the raven. Despite this, Dad strode towards the ring. To anyone else, Dad looked just like the other wrestlers who had appeared that evening, but to Jake's trained eye, this wasn't the fighter he knew. Dad looked nervous and edgy, two words not in his wrestling dictionary.

'Why isn't he snarling?' Jake muttered to himself. 'And why are the crowd *eating* their pizza instead of slinging it at him?' But there was no one to answer his fears, so he concentrated on the big screen. Hang on? What was that music? What the—?

Arnie McBride had even changed Dad's theme tune! Instead of Jake's thrashing guitars, Dad was entering the ring to the sound of *Land of Hope and Glory*! Jake HATED that song. They had to sing it at school occasionally, and it was one of those irritating tunes where everyone belted out the first line, only to mumble the rest because they didn't have the foggiest how it went.

And that's just what was happening tonight.

The crowd, blissfully unaware that every single thing about Dad's wrestling persona had changed, went nuts!

'LAND OF HO-OPE AND GLOOO-RY!' they sang, before whispering, 'Mehmeeh la-de-da-doooo!'

'What's going on?' shouted Mouse over the noise. 'Where's my costume?'

'I don't know,' said Jake.

'You could've told me, you know, if they thought it was rubbish.'

'*I* didn't know either, mate, honest!'

Dad had reached the ring now, but instead of stepping

effortlessly over the top rope as he usually did, he dipped his head and ducked in between them. If ever there was evidence that things were about to go horribly wrong, then that insignificant moment summed it up. Dad *always* strode over the top rope. It reminded his opponents what a man mountain they were facing. What on earth was Dad thinking?

Suddenly, though, the screen went dark. And stayed dark. Jake felt overwhelming relief. Maybe there'd been a power cut? Or Arnie McBride had realised he'd made a terrible mistake and had cancelled the whole thing.

His joy was short-lived. A deafening, sinister laugh echoed through the speakers: an unspeakable noise that sounded as though it had rumbled all the way up from hell.

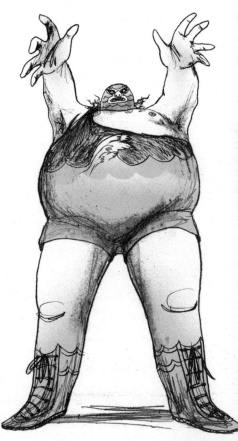

Then – WHAM! – a lightning flash ripped across the screen, and there, in the middle of the ring, arms stretched wide, stood the beast that was The Tsunami Terror. Jake felt daft. Of course it wasn't a power cut – The Terror always entered the ring like this.

The camera zoomed in. The Terror's eyes were cold and lifeless, his limbs ready to inflict maximum pain. Jake didn't think it was possible to feel any more scared, until – *WHAM!* – (again), the Terror clapped his hands, and lightning zapped between his palms. Lightning. I promise you. A blue, fizzing bolt that could set the whole world ablaze. Now the Terror was pointing at Dad, electricity still rippling off his fingertips.

'DOOOOOOM . . .' The Terror mouthed at Dad. 'DOOOOOOOOOOOM.'

Jake saw a bead of sweat break across his Dad's forehead. Then another, and another.

'Oh boy,' Jake whimpered. 'Oh boy, oh boy, oh boy.' This wasn't in the script, but it was definitely happening.

16
The Tidal Wave...

Jake barely heard the introductions over the roaring of the crowd and the screaming in his head. Unlike Jake, the crowd had no idea just how badly wrong things had already gone.

'Look at the weight he's lost!' gasped one woman, who was wearing a matching George Biggs T-shirt and headband set.

'He looks amazing!' yelled her husband, waving a pair of huge foam hands. 'He'll be quicker now. Maybe *too* quick for the Terror.'

Jake wanted to stick the foam hands up the man's nostrils. the Demolition Man had been the only wrestler in the world big enough to match the Terror's power. The Beefeater might be quicker, with greater stamina, but had Dad had enough training time to get used to his new physique? And did he know how to use it without Jake there to coach him?

Jake had no option but to hope so. To wish dearly that whatever expert training he'd had was about to come off!

'Have you ever seen him look like that?' he asked Mum, equally transfixed by the screen.

'Not since we met,' she replied dreamily. 'He looks like a

million quid.' It wasn't often that wrestling impressed her, but tonight it DEFINITELY did.

A hush fell over the crowd as the introductions were made in the ring.

It didn't escape Jake's attention that when the announcer wailed out Dad's new wrestling name, 'The Priiiiiide of ENGERLAND – The BEEFEATER, GEORGEEEEY BEEEEEE,' Dad didn't seem to realise they were even talking about him. And actually, Jake wasn't sure Dad had ever seen a Beefeater before. Beefeaters lived in London, and all the noise and hullaballoo down there gave people from Seacross nosebleeds if they dared go that far south.

It was only when Dad heard the Las Vegas crowds roaring their approval that he reluctantly held his arms aloft. To Jake, this didn't look like the action of a confident warrior off to battle. Far from it . . .

'Arnie probably doesn't realise Seacross is nowhere near London,' Floss shouted. 'He probably thinks it's just down the road!'

Finally, and to the dismay of an increasingly panicky Jake, the bell rang. The match had started. The match Jake had made happen. The match of his dreams. Or was it his nightmares?

No sooner had the bell stopped echoing, than the Terror crossed the ring in a single stride and was in Dad's face. But strangely, once there he did nothing, just stood stock-still and stared straight into Dad's eyes.

'MOVE!' yelled Jake, fearing a venomous swipe at any second, 'For goodness sake, Dad, MOVE!'

Suddenly Dad seemed to hear the crowd baying at him to fight. With a flourish, he pulled back his left arm, and – *WHAM!* – connected with a slap, flush on the Terror's cheek.

'Here we go!' yelled Jake.

'Is that the blow that signals the beginning of the end for our fearsome champion . . .?' gasped Tiger from the commentary box.

But the Terror didn't move, not an inch. It was as if someone had tried to cut down a giant oak tree with a butter knife. Then he threw back his head and howled with laughter. A laugh that said, 'Is that all you've got?'

George danced to his left. Suddenly, with a howl, the Terror grabbed hold of Dad's shoulders and, with the merest flick, hoisted him above his head.

The Seacross crowd gasped as one. Advice rolled from every mouth.

'Punch him . . .'

'Nip him . . .'

'Give him a Chinese burn!'

But Dad was helpless. All he could do was yelp as the champion launched him across the ring, straight into the post in Dad's corner.

Jake wished more than anything that he was ringside, where he could shout in Dad's ear. He caught sight of Arnie on the front row a few times, hollering advice in Dad's direction. But it didn't look as if Dad could hear him.

The Terror was the only one thinking clearly, lifting Dad by the ears this time, before dropping him flat onto his bent knee.

'Backbreaker!!' yelled Tiger, with too much pleasure for Jake's liking. 'That's gotta hurt!'

There was no hiding place. Every time George hit the deck, there was the Terror, stalking him, lifting him, inflicting upon him every single wrestling move known to man.

SUPLEX!

PILEDRIVER!

CLOTHESLINE!

Jake was seriously scared now, tears gathering in his eyes. Mum's confidence had dissolved too, as she yelled,

'STOP THE FIGHT!'

She'd covered Lewis's eyes after the first mighty throw, holding on for dear life as he wriggled like an eel. But as matters in the ring got worse, Mum needed to cover Lewis's ears too. Because a few idiots in the hall started to get on Dad's back.

'What is he doing?' yelled one.

'Fight back!' shouted another.

Jake felt his cheeks flush as Mouse and Floss tried to defend Dad from the insults.

'We'd like to see you do better.'

'Yeah, you couldn't fight a cold . . . '

Admirable, of course, but who ever listened to little kids?

Back in Vegas, the Terror looked peckish. Not that he was going to get much meat off George's left ear.

'Ooooooh!' cried Tiger. 'Someone pass the champ some
ketchup!'

On and on the torture went. Dad was folded more times than
an origami swan. The Terror was too big and too strong for the
Beefeater: he didn't have a thing to throw back at him. Where

were his moves? thought Jake. What about all the training he'd been doing these past weeks in America?

Suddenly it hit Jake – there was one thing Dad could try, one thing that had never, ever let him down in the ring: The Wrecking Ball.

Jake closed his eyes, as tight as he possibly could, and sent the strongest psychic message to Dad, all those thousands of miles away. *Do it, Dad, do it!* He daren't open them again, he daren't. Until he heard the crowd gasp . . .

'What's he doing with his arm?'

'Why is he swinging it like that?'

'Maybe he's so punch drunk he thinks he's a helicopter . . . '

But Jake knew what was happening. He opened his eyes. Dad was winding up his left arm. He'd heard him! Somehow, Dad had really heard him! He was preparing the Wrecking Ball!

In a flash, Jake was jumping in the air, and so were Mouse and Floss.

Faster and faster Dad's arm spun, so fast a breeze seemed to pass through City Hall. The momentum propelled Dad towards the champ . . . it was going to work, it really was. This was it—

Or maybe not. Because just as Dad's fist came within an inch of the Terror's chin, the champion side-stepped like a ballet dancer, and with grace and speed and power, lifted Dad clean into the air, before slamming him, full force, down onto the mat.

'TEN-TON TIDAL WAVE!!!' yelled Tiger. 'There'll be no way back from that . . . GOOODNIGHT, LONDON!!!'

And the commentator was right, as the Tsunami Terror threw his full body weight on Dad from the top rope, leaving the ref to start counting the pin-fall.

'ONE . . . TWO . . . THREE!'

That was it. Fight over.

Just not in the way Jake had dreamed.

Demolition Done . . .

The next thirty minutes were not a happy time for young Jake Biggs.

I'd rather not tell you about it, to be honest; it's all a bit upsetting and I rather like Jake, just as you do. But if I gloss over the bad stuff then you might get cross with me and take this book back to the shop, even though you've bent the spine already and folded the pages over instead of using a bookmark (tut tut!). Anyway, I don't want you to ask for a refund, so I'll tell you what happened next.

I promise.

Ready?

Good.

The next thirty minutes were not a happy ti— Oh, sorry, I've done that already . . . Er, yep, OK.

Jake had never had a worse thirty minutes in his life. Even the death of his beloved gerbil, Nibbles, who had perished eating a piece of Lego, didn't come close.

The capacity crowd in City Hall was devastated but, worse than that, some of them were angry too.

'What a waste of time,' one man moaned to his wife.

'Makes us look like a right bunch of losers, doesn't it?'

'I've seen trifles with more backbone!'

There was one group of people more upset than the others. They were booing, tearing up their foam hands and throwing the pieces at the screen. They were, of course, the Milner clan, and their equally horrible friends.

'Proud of him, are you . . .?' snarled Masher, sneaking up on Jake while Mum was out of earshot.

'Leave it, Masher,' said Floss.

'No, I won't leave it. Do you have any idea how much business my dad might lose because of this? The Beefeater is going to cost us big time.'

'If it wasn't for his dad, there wouldn't have been any business *to* lose, you idiot,' Floss snapped back.

'Tell that to my uncle over there. He's got a multi-million-pound contract to build that theme park for Arnie McBride.

Not going to happen now, though, is it?'

'He did his best,' Jake said. 'If he hadn't lost all that weight he would've flattened the Terror.'

'If he hadn't lost all that weight, he'd have been popped like a zit.'

Masher saw Jake's mum heading their way, her face like thunder.

'Keep looking over your shoulder, Biggs,' he whispered menacingly. 'I wouldn't go to sleep if I were you.'

'Was he bothering you?' Mum asked, as she tried to steer Jake towards the exit.

But Jake didn't want to leave, not yet. Not until he knew Dad was OK.

After what felt like a million agonising slow-motion replays, he finally caught a glimpse of Dad stumbling through the braying Vegas crowd, alongside a frowning Arnie McBride. It didn't make him feel any better.

Worries piled on top of worries, all the way home in the limo.

Dad looked totally humiliated. Was he OK?

Would he be angry that I made him go to America?

Why couldn't I just have kept it our secret?

And what about Mum? Would Arnie still fly her to a six-star hotel in outer space when The Beefeater had turned out to be vegetarian?

Jake couldn't bear the thought of Mum's dreams disappearing too. He knew how excited she'd been about the chance to travel again. She deserved that trip; she was the best mum he could ask for.

'I'm so sorry, Mum,' he said, trying not to cry. 'This is all my fault.'

Mum slipped her arm around him and squeezed tenderly.

'Don't be silly. There's nothing wrong with wanting the world to see what you see. You had good intentions, that's what matters. Dad'll be OK.'

'I just don't understand what happened. Why did Arnie change everything about Dad when the Demolition Man was already so brilliant?'

'I don't know, Jake. I just don't know. I'm hardly an expert. But Dad had a bloomin' good go. And he's still your dad, you can still be proud.'

Jake was proud, but he was frustrated too, and as much as he hated to admit it, a little bit embarrassed. And confused. How could he feel so many different things all at once?

'It wouldn't have happened if I'd been there with him. Won't be happening next time either. There'll be none of this Beefeater business. First thing we need to do when Dad gets home is feed him, get some meat back on his bones—'

'Hold on, Jake, love. Next time?' said Mum. 'Do you really think Dad will want there to be a next time?'

Jake opened his mouth, but nothing came out. It was a knockout blow. There had to be a next time. It was just like Dad always said. All fighters get beaten every now and then. What makes them a champ is how they get up again . . .

Jake wanted to tell Mum that, to ask if she believed it. But he knew she wouldn't have the answer. The person who did was thousands of miles away, nursing a bruised body and a ruptured dream.

He'd call Dad the second he got home.

18

The Morning After the Night Before

What's the worst noise in the world?

The silent rattle of an empty moneybox?

A motley choir of foxes singing a One Direction song in your back garden at 3.39 a.m.?

Or even One Direction singing a One Direction song. The agony!

Well, none of these got even close to the repetitive sound of Dad's voicemail message.

Jake knew this because he'd been ringing him from the moment he got home until he'd passed out long after dawn. When he woke, shortly after midday on Sunday, he not only owned a phone-indented cheek, but a handset covered in saliva.

He wasted no time in dashing downstairs to Mum.

'Has he called you?' Jake said.

'Who?' Mum was shoving armfuls of washing into the machine. 'David Beckham? George Clooney? Strangely, both of them have – with separate proposals of marriage. I've asked them to write me 500-word essays on why I should say yes.' She stared dreamily into the distance. 'Can't imagine David will come up

with much. Maybe I'll see who
can do the most press-ups instead.'

Jake had NO idea what Mum was talking about. Sometimes he really didn't understand adults, which was why he'd sworn never to turn into one.

'Eh?' he said. 'I mean Dad. Has Dad called?'

This pulled Mum back to reality. Back to the fact that she was just as worried as Jake.

'Oh. Yes. He has,' she said, turning back to the washing.

'And?' Jake said. Honestly, Mum could be so frustrating.

'Well, he's as you'd expect, love. Tired and bruised and disappoint—'

'But he is OK, isn't he?'

'Why don't you speak to him?' Mum said.

Jake reached for her phone.

'Not now, he'll be in bed!'

'But you said to call him!'

'Look, just let him sleep for now. I know you're upset, and I know you're worried, but calling him at four in the morning isn't going to change anything. I wish it would, but it won't. Call him in a bit, eh?'

She was right, of course. (Mums usually are.) It was far too early. So Jake got dressed, and went outside instead.

It was quiet on Storey Street - little wonder after everyone's late night. Curtains were drawn, tellies turned off. There wasn't a single person out washing their car.

Jake headed for The House That Was Stolen. He needed to think. He sat on the sofa and turned on the TV with the imaginary remote control. He stared at the screen, trying to make sense of what had happened, and what it meant for them.

Had Arnie always intended Dad to lose?

But *why* would he want that?

Was it likely that Arnie would give Dad a second chance?

And even if he did, would Dad want to get back in the ring ever again?

Jake was sitting, lost in his own thoughts, when an upstairs window opened on the house next door, and a familiar face loomed into view.

Well, a nose came first. A nose so broken in fights and rugby matches that it looked like a wonky Cumberland sausage. It was attached to the face of Masher Milner.

Jake groaned. He'd been so preoccupied with Dad, he hadn't realised what a dumb place this was to hang out today. This was only going to end in one way – pain.

'Oi, loser, son of loser. Get off our land.'

Masher always claimed that The House That Was Stolen belonged to them, though the truth was no one knew who owned it. It was one of life's great mysteries, like 'Why were sprouts invented when they taste so rank?'

Jake cupped a hand to his ear, then pointed to the telly, as if he couldn't hear. He knew he should've walked away, but he didn't care today. How could he when his pride was already so bruised?

'I said, OI, LOSER!' Every window frame on the street shook. Dogs whimpered in their baskets. 'What part of that don't you compute?'

The insult echoed in Jake's head. If Masher was going to make his life a misery, he might as well start now. Let him do his worst. After all, it couldn't be any more painful than what had already happened.

'I didn't realise you owned this place too, Quentin,' Jake said. Talk about brave! No one called Masher by his real name – not the teachers at school, not his parents, not even his own grandma.

'Don't get lippy, soft lad,' Masher roared. 'Not after what your old man did last night.'

'What?' said Jake. 'Having the bravery to get in the ring with the most fearsome fighter in the world? I didn't see *your* dad doing that . . . '

Quen— I mean Masher - didn't like the suggestion that his dear dad was a wimp (not when he was the most successful estate agent in the whole of Seacross), and with one swift movement, he pulled himself clean out of the window and shimmied down the drainpipe.

Oh boy! yelled a voice in Jake's head. Whose stupid idea was this? Was he *really* going to square up to this maniac?

'You want to talk about my dad?' the bully shouted, striding towards Jake. 'My old man's got three offices in Seacross and a fleet of Minis. Minis that would have been Rolls-Royces if it wasn't for your dad,' said Masher, shoving Jake's chest.

'Yeah, well, *my* dad's in Las Vegas, in a suite on the sixty-fifth floor!' Jake didn't really know if that was a good floor to be on, but it sounded high up, at least.

'After the pasting he took last night, your old man is probably in hospital. You should call the nurses, see if they can inject him with some backbone.'

'That the best you can do?' Jake answered, though inside, the insult stung.

'Oh, I can do WAY better than that. Your old man's a coward and a fake. He ran around that ring like the world's biggest loser, only weeks after standing on stage, telling the world just how great he was. You and him spun the biggest lie this town's ever heard.'

Jake's knees quivered. It was like having his darkest thoughts read out loud. But Masher wasn't finished.

'Now I don't care if your dad's a loser – it's not as if we've learned anything new, is it? But what I do care about is you making *us* look stupid too. Us that live here. The whole world isn't just laughing at you and your dad, they're laughing at us too!'

Jake felt his insides begin to prickle. He was finding it difficult to breathe. It was as if Masher's hands were around his neck, squeezing tight. He had no comeback, nothing to put him in his place. He raised his hands into fists. If he had to fight Masher, then he'd do it. He'd do it for his dad.

The bully laughed and paced menacingly forward. Jake winced in anticipation. He wanted to be brave, but it was difficult when he knew it was going to really hurt.

As Masher's fist flashed forward, Jake felt someone yank him backwards. Masher, with no one there to cushion his fist, crashed clumsily to the ground.

Jake spun round to find his two best pals with determined looks on their faces.

'What are you doing?!' yelled Mouse, as he pulled Jake away. 'What sort of a mentalist are you?'

Floss stood over the groaning Masher.

'Oi, you,' she shouted. 'You want to rearrange anyone's face, then come and have a go at me. See how tough everyone thinks you are then, eh?'

And with her head held high, she led Mouse and Jake back to the safety of the Biggs's house.

'Thank you!' Jake said, his voice trembling. 'I kind of like the way my face looks.' Though as he peered back towards a growling Masher, he wasn't sure he'd be able to protect his nose for long.

19

A Glorious Homecoming ...

The airport was emptier than a dietician's biscuit barrel, a painful contrast to the scenes when Dad had left for America. Gone were the crowds and the chanting, and there was certainly no crowd surfing – only tired travellers pulling their wheelie-bags behind them.

Jake pasted his smile on, determined to make this a happy homecoming for Dad.

The four days since Grapplemania had been torturous, but Jake had known it was up to him to turn the situation around.

Dad hadn't become a terrible wrestler overnight – it was just one fight. He had to convince Arnie McBride. Persuade him to give Dad another chance. He might have to persuade Dad too!

The first problem was that Arnie wasn't easy to pin down. His phone calls had been ignored. As were texts and emails. It wasn't until Jake went slightly loopy and emailed, texted and called the American every minute that Arnie finally picked up the phone.

'What *DO* you want?' he yelled. 'You're acting like my seventh wife did before she mysteriously disappeared.'

Not exactly the start Jake had been hoping for, so he tried to play it cool.

'Just a chat really, Mr McBride, you know, to see what's next for Dad.'

'Next?'

'Er, yeah, you know, now Grapplemania is over.'

There was a pause. 'Look, last I heard your daddy was on the plane home. He's going to need to ice those bruises and get himself back to work.'

This was brilliant, thought Jake. Arnie was already lining up the next fight!

'Fantastic! When will that be?'

'Well, that's up to his boss, isn't it? I guess as soon as your daddy can walk properly again.'

Eh? 'No, not *that* work,' Jake said. 'I meant, when's his next fight with *WOW!*?'

'Son, there ain't going to be no more fights. Not with me, not with *WOW!* Not after what went on in Vegas.'

'You're kidding?' Jake couldn't let it sound as if he'd half expected to hear this.

'Do I sound like I'm laughing?'

'Well, no, but—'

'But nothing. It's over, son. Move on.'

This was crazy. If Dad hadn't fought well in Vegas, there was only one person to blame.

'But, Mr McBride, there are reasons for what happened at Grapplemania. I mean, you changed Dad's fighting persona at the last minute, then made him lose all that weight. Then there was the music and the bird and—'

'Whoa, whoa, whoa,' Arnie boomed. 'Let's get one thing straight. I gave your daddy and that one-horse town of yours the best opportunity they've ever had. I gave your dad the chance to put Seacross on the map, to become the centre of the wrestling universe. All he had to do was come out and put on a show! But he couldn't do that, could he?'

'He *could've* done if you hadn't changed everything about him.'

'You think I forced your daddy to change all those things? Son, your dad couldn't WAIT to drop that dumb costume and act. You think he enjoyed looking like a soggy blancmange? No way! I gave him the tools; he just didn't know how to use 'em.'

Jake didn't believe that, not a word of it, but he could tell arguing was pointless. Instead he went for good old-fashioned begging.

'Give him a second chance. Please? I'll sharpen him up. Have him bouncing opponents off the ceiling in weeks.'

'I don't think so, boy. I spent millions planning this competition. I gave him the best trainers, the best nutritionists. I was going to make wrestling as big as football in your tin-pot country, and your daddy ruined it. Thanks to your dad, there'll be no wrestling theme park and certainly no George Biggs museum. I mean, who on earth would visit *that?* Son, it's over. And so is this phone call.'

'No . . . Wait!' Jake said. But the line went dead. Jake had to accept the truth. The *WOW!* dream was over as quickly as it had begun.

Which brings us back to the airport, where Jake, Mum and Lewis were waiting to welcome Dad back in style.

To Jake, despite everything, Dad was still a hero, just for getting up there and fighting a wrestling legend, regardless of what Arnie or Masher said. Jake had stayed up late two nights running to paint a banner to hold at the arrivals gate.

'Welcome Home, Champ!' it read, lovingly painted in bright red paint.

It had been a rush to get it finished, but Jake didn't mind. He'd pinned it on the washing line to dry overnight, before rolling it up in a rush as they dashed for the airport.

OK, so Grapplemania hadn't gone well. But the important thing was that Dad was coming home, and Jake was going to dedicate every hour of the day to showing him how proud he was.

Mum, Lewis and Jake waited by the arrivals gate, banner in hand. An hour later, they were *still* waiting, Jake irritated by the endless stream of passengers grinning at his sign.

'Where's Daddy?' Lewis wailed for the millionth time, but Mum hadn't a clue, and was none the wiser after double-checking that Dad's plane had actually landed. They were about to give up and go home, when the arrival door slid open and . . .

'DAAAAD!' Jake and Lewis yelled. They turned their smiles up to full beam, and held the banner high.

Dad stopped dead, the doors jamming shut against his luggage trolley. His eyes flitted across Jake's banner.

But something was wrong. Why wasn't he smiling? Why wasn't he pleased? It was a simple, honest message. It was supposed to make his day.

Jake turned to look at the banner and got a shock. It still said three simple words – with one tiny, fundamental difference. The 'a' in champ had been tampered with – 'Champ' had become 'Chump'.

Jake didn't know whether to be angry or burst into tears. He knew instantly who was responsible. It had Masher's vengeful hands stamped all over it. He must have spotted it drying on the line. Why hadn't he hung it in his room?

Jake dashed towards Dad, ready to explain it was a just a stupid, spiteful prank. But as he got closer, he saw the full horror on Dad's face. He was wearing the same hurt expression he had when he'd stumbled from the Las Vegas ring.

'I didn't write that. Someone's set me up. It's their idea of a joke,' cried Jake.

'And a good one,' Dad answered sadly.

'It wasn't me who wrote it, Dad, honest!'

'Doesn't matter who wrote it,' said Dad. 'We should frame it. They've got it spot on.'

Pancakes, Anyone?

The car journey home from the airport was quiet, quieter than the silent rattle of an empty money box.

What? I've used that one already? Well, you'll know what I mean then, won't you? It was quiet. Proper, deathly quiet.

After settling himself in the passenger seat, Dad had barely said a word, though Jake noticed him flinch repeatedly when he saw his face beaming down from roadside billboards. Where was his usual smile? Where were the stories from America? Jake watched him, troubled.

The car pulled into Storey Street, which was buzzing with activity as always. Cars were being washed, gates painted, games of football played in the middle of the road. Dad slid down into his seat, as if trying not to be seen.

He had to get out of the car eventually though, and as he opened the door, Mouse and Floss ran to say hello, forcing a smile onto Dad's face.

Dad looked down the street as if he hadn't seen it in years, waved weakly at a handful of neighbours peering nosily over their front fence, before lugging his suitcase up the path.

As the front door closed behind them, they heard something

explode against it. Jake peeped through the letterbox, only for a second object to hit it.

'Eggs,' he gasped, 'someone's throwing eggs!'

Mum ran to the front window, but couldn't spot the culprit. 'Kids,' she huffed. 'I'll be having words with their parents if I spot them.'

Jake was pretty sure he knew who it was. 'Don't worry, Mum,' he said, smiling at Dad. 'Couple more and we'll have enough for pancakes.'

The old Dad would have laughed at this, or licked his lips at the mention of food. But this Dad didn't – there wasn't even a flicker of a grin or the tiniest of tummy rumbles.

Instead he shrugged and started pulling his wheelie case forlornly up the stairs. Every bump felt like a nail being hammered further and further into Jake's heart.

The rest of the day was odd. Dad slumped in the lounge, staring at a TV that wasn't switched on, drowning in clothes that had once fitted him snugly. Jake sat with him for a while, trying to spark a conversation, but nothing worked.

'Shall we go out today, Dad?'

'I could do with a rest, son.'

'Maybe we could watch a film then?'

'Yeah . . . later, eh?'

What made it even weirder for Jake was that this was Saturday. Wrestling day. Right now they would usually be in the van, talking tactics, gearing up for a fight. But today, Dad couldn't even fight his way out of the armchair.

What had they done to him over there? What had Jake got him into?

George didn't mention the eggs that still flew intermittently at the door, but Jake knew they must have been on his mind. It wasn't the sort of thing you could ignore. Later, Jake scrubbed the front door (eggs didn't half stink when the sun started cooking them), while Dad pretended to unpack, though every time Jake went up to try and tempt him with a cup of tea or a snack, he found Dad lying on the bed, his back to the door, staring out of the window. More worryingly, he didn't touch *any* of the food Jake took him. Not even the peanut butter and chocolate cookies Jake had made especially for his homecoming.

By bedtime, Jake felt as if he was in the middle of a film where father and son swap bodies.

'You really should eat something, Dad.'

'What, and risk my six pack?' Dad replied glumly.

Jake admired the attempt at a joke, but he could tell Dad's heart wasn't in it. Being skinny didn't suit him and they both knew it.

'It won't help, you know, losing all this weight.' He didn't want to bring up wrestling, but Dad had refused to talk about anything else, and Jake was feeling desperate.

'Course it will. Clothes will be a lot cheaper if there's half as much material.'

'You know what I mean.'

Dad said nothing.

Jake tried again. 'It's not that bad, Dad, what happened over there. Not many people would dare get in the ring with that lunatic!'

'I messed it up though, didn't I? What must everyone think of me? They must be killing themselves laughing.'

'Of course they're not. And anyway, it doesn't matter what they think. They don't understand wrestling. Everyone has to lose at some point. And anyway, it's not about how you get knocked down, it's how you get back up again, isn't that right?'

'But what if you don't want to get up again? What if you can't?' Dad said, with a sigh.

Jake was worried. He'd never heard Dad like this before. He sounded so defeated. He searched his head for the right thing to say, but hadn't a clue. He was almost relieved when Mum appeared, her hand resting gently on his shoulder.

'Come on, Jake,' she said. 'Bedtime.'

'Can't I sit here a while? Dad could read to me.'

Mum glanced at Dad. 'Tomorrow, maybe. Your dad's tired. He needs to sleep.'

Reluctantly, and after a limp hug from Dad, Jake did as he was told.

Mum told him and Lewis a story. Jake knew he shouldn't have been disappointed: after all, Mum's tales had always been the best. But tonight, more than ever, all Jake really wanted was his dad.

21

The Walls Come Tumbling Down...

Dad didn't do a lot the next day.

Mum made him get dressed, but no amount of cajoling could force him from the house. Instead he wandered slowly from room to room, lost in his thoughts.

Now Jake didn't know much about jet lag, but he was pretty sure it made people feel tired rather than unhappy.

He spied on Dad from the doorway of his room, saw him staring zombie-like at the wall.

Monday morning offered a small slither of hope, because Dad was due back at work. When Dad had won the competition, Jake never dreamed that he would be going back to his old job, but Dad had refused to hand in his notice.

'I haven't won yet,' he'd said. 'We might still need the money when I get back.' His boss, delighted to be associated with such a famous man, had gifted Dad the extra holiday.

And now, of course, with the dream of a wrestling career more tattered than a tramp's sock, there wasn't any other option. It became very clear, however, that the reality of life back on the demolition site wasn't something Dad felt ready to face.

There was no sign of him at the breakfast table at seven-thirty, eight or eight-thirty. In the end, Mum had to go upstairs and talk him down. Well, it started as talk, but after twenty minutes, it turned into a shout, then a yell until finally, a reluctant Dad appeared, dressed for work. It felt like a momentous moment – he'd been wearing his pyjamas all weekend – so this was a BIG improvement.

He sat at the table in silence, stirring a volcanically hot cup of tea for so long Jake worried the spoon might melt. Mum scowled at his delaying tactics and poured the brew down the sink.

Jake thought he knew what was going on in her head. It was the same thing that was going on in his.

OK, so the promise of a glamorous trip around the world (and definitely the one into outer space) might have disappeared, but Mum could live with that. What bothered her more was that someone seemed to have kidnapped her husband's fighting spirit.

Now, instead of having two children to clear up after, she seemed to have a third too. Even though she looked cross, Jake knew she was sad as well. Sad and, more importantly, worried.

Time for Jake to step in. After all, this was *his* fault.

'Why don't I come to work with you today, Dad?' he said brightly. 'I've no school for weeks, so there's nothing else to do.'

Dad usually loved it when Jake joined him on site. Loved showing his boy off to his mates. Even today, he smiled at the prospect, though Jake could see it was a struggle to make it look real.

It was enough for Jake, who took it as a yes and went to fetch George's steel toe-capped boots. They were probably the only item in his wardrobe that still fitted him.

Fifteen minutes later, after shoehorning Dad out of the door, they were off. Jake was carrying a hamper the size of a bungalow, hoping a few hours of destruction would give Dad an appetite and snap him out of this strange mood.

But as they left the house, things didn't go to plan. Masher had given up egg slinging and decided to step up the torment levels. And strangely, for a bully with an IQ of minus 159, he did it cleverly. He tailed Dad and Jake all the way to work without being spotted, and every thirty seconds, performed a loud impression of a chicken clucking. This might not sound like much to you, but to a paranoid dad and his worried son, well, it started to get under their skin. After five minutes of it, Dad was looking over his shoulder. After ten minutes, he looked like he wanted to turn round and run home.

Finally Dad stood at the site gates, eyes flitting over the job in hand – two ancient blocks of flats that sat a short distance from a new, gleaming modern tower. Locals called these old buildings the 'Ugly Sisters'.

'Won't take you long to take them down, Dad,' said Jake. And it was true. Dad swatted wrecks like this before breakfast usually. It was just what he needed, Jake thought – a taste of normality, a reminder of his immense skills.

Dad didn't look so sure. A bead of sweat trickled down the side of his face. He looked even sweatier when a number of his work mates spotted him.

'George!' they cried, mischief etched on their faces.

'Welcome back.'

'How was America?'

'Hard luck with the result . . . '

Dad, normally one of the gang, didn't know how to react. Words scrambled in his head, he couldn't look them in the eye.

'Listen,' said one man, who Jake recognised as one of the bosses, Davey O'Callaghan. 'There've been some new rules passed while you were away. Health and Safety. New uniforms. You know how it is . . . '

And with that, he pulled out a bright yellow helmet with a Beefeater's hat wedged on the top. He thrust it onto Dad's head and banged it into place, to the delight of the other workers.

'Ha ha,' said Jake. 'Very funny.' He hoped Dad would come back with a response of his own. He was well used to this kind of banter, after all. But he remained silent and uncomfortable.

Jake tried to steer Dad away, but the lads weren't quite finished.

'Oh, and George?' yelled Davey. 'There's a new lad on site. Work experience kid. Wants to work with the best, so we've paired him up with you.'

With a flourish, he pulled from his overalls the most pathetic

137

excuse for a stuffed bird Jake had ever seen. It didn't look like a raven. It wasn't even black, although they had tried to dip it in something. Tar maybe.

Roughly, he stuck it to Dad's shoulder and howled with laughter. Dad looked as if he was about to die with shame.

Jake's pulse was going mental. First Masher, now this.

Why wouldn't anyone give Dad a break?

'Oh yeah, you can laugh.' Jake yelled. 'But I don't remember any of you queuing up to fight the toughest wrestler in the world. So if you haven't tried it, don't knock it!'

He hoped it might quieten them down enough to get Dad out of earshot, but they just laughed harder.

'Ignore them, Dad,' Jake said, throwing the bird into the nearest skip. He'd have done the same to the Beefeater's hat if he could reach Dad's head.

'Tell you what. Shall I come into the cab with you?'

That way he could encourage Dad, remind him how good he was. 'Been a while since I sat with you up there.'

'Sure,' Dad said.

It took them an age to climb the long ladder. Dad kept glancing down and closing his eyes, as if in fear. *Both* of them were nervous by the time they were sitting, side by side, in the cab. Below, Jake could see Dad's workmates still laughing among themselves. Dad could see it too, and Jake was sure it was doing nothing for his state of mind.

'It's OK,' said Jake. 'You can do this, Dad, easy. You're the greatest.'

George fired the engine up, but as the vibrations cut through the cab, his fingers didn't move.

'What's wrong?' Jake shouted over the noise.

'I can't do it,' whispered Dad. He seemed to whisper everything these days.

'Pardon?'

'I said I can't do it. Not today,'

'Is it because of what they just said? Ignore them, they're idiots!'

Jake had seen him knock down bigger buildings with a mere flick of his wrist, but what happened in Vegas seemed to have destroyed the Dad he knew.

Dad nodded, then shook his head. He clearly didn't know what was going on in that brain of his.

'Just ignore them. I believe in you. Mum and Lewis do too. And Mouse and Floss. Those idiots down there will be ribbing someone else tomorrow – you know how it works.'

It was true, Jake knew it was, but it didn't seem to do anything to help Dad, who sat there, motionless.

So started a not so merry dance, which involved Jake putting Dad's hands on the controls, and like a ventriloquist's dummy, trying to get George to move the wrecking ball towards the Ugly Sisters. Jake had never done this before, not without Dad being in real control, and all ventriloquists are a bit rubbish when they first start. They can't even say 'gottle of geer', I mean, 'bottle of beer'.

Dad was in a right old state now, sweat pouring so freely you'd think he was sitting beneath a waterfall. His hands were clammy and shaking so badly that they kept slipping off the controls.

'It's OK, Dad,' Jake said, although it clearly wasn't. Dad didn't even seem to be looking at the building any more.

Reluctantly, Jake turned off the engine. The wrecking ball swung sadly, until, like a badly wound grandfather clock, it came to a halt. Jake had no option but to return with Dad, defeated, to the ground.

Jake followed Dad past his workmates. They weren't laughing any more. They looked confused. George Biggs NEVER left a building standing. Never.

'George!' they yelled.

'George, where are you going?'

'What shall we tell the boss?'

Jake looked at Dad, his lovely dad. He was still shaking, tears forming in his eyes. What was happening to him?

'Tell him whatever you like,' Jake said. 'We're going home.'

22
Mum Spreads Her Wings...

After that, things in the Biggs household took a turn for the worse.

Hard to believe, dear reader, but true. Imagine being in a zoo, and thinking you're heading for the café, only to find you've followed signs to the lion enclosure (without a car or rifle for protection). That's the kind of turn we're talking about.

When they got home, Dad went straight upstairs to his bedroom. He didn't go back to work on Tuesday, or Wednesday. Finally, after much persuading from Mum, Dad rang work and arranged to be taken off demolition duties for a while. His boss didn't like it, but agreed that Dad could work as a labourer, clearing away rubble and making tea, as long as he took a pay cut. Jake didn't understand what was going on. How could Dad not want to demolish stuff when he was just SO good at it?

'You see?' said Mum, as Dad put down the phone. 'I told you he'd be OK about it.'

Dad looked relieved, but only for a moment, as Mum went on.

'Now you've done that you can get yourself dressed and put your shoes on.'

'Why? Where are we going?'

'To see the doctor. If you're not feeling well, George, let's nip it in the bud now.'

On their return an hour later, Jake saw that Dad was carrying a small paper bag packed full with vitamins. Jake hoped they were strong enough to make him happy again.

After Dad plonked himself miserably in front of the telly, Jake turned to Mum.

'What did the doctor say? Is it a bug or a virus – what?'

Mum sighed. 'No, no son, it's nothing for you to be worrying about. Your dad's tired, and a bit stressed. He's been through a lot this past few weeks.'

Jake exhaled noisily. It was a bit of a relief, to be honest.

'So what can I do then? To make him feel better?'

Mum hugged Jake softly. 'Same thing you always do. Be kind to him, make him laugh. We have to let him rest when he's tired, but the doctor said fresh air would help as well. So let's keep him busy.'

'Work will do that, won't it? Maybe Dad should get back behind the wrecking ball after all?'

'Let's not push it, Jake. If it's stressing Dad out, then it's best he stays on the site floor for a while.'

Jake didn't like this. First the wrestling had gone wrong, now the demolition too. How could Dad possibly feel happy without two of the things he was good at? Another worry flashed into his head too, one he couldn't keep in.

'What about money, Mum? If Dad's taken a pay cut, what do we do about that?'

Mum squeezed harder.

'Don't you worry about that. We'll figure something out.'

But Jake wasn't daft, and he wasn't a kid either: he was nearly eleven for goodness sake. It only took a few weeks for him to realise that money really *was* tighter than normal. He could see it in the food they were eating. Ham wasn't coming in slices any more; it came in a tin, coated in a thick jelly that made Jake gag. Vegetables came in tins too – green beans limper than a one-legged pirate without a crutch.

It started to affect Jake in other ways too, like school. Autumn term had begun, the perfect opportunity for Masher to find another level of torture.

'Setting a new fashion trend, loser?' he yelled, pointing at Jake's trousers, which were so short they barely covered his socks. He knew he should've asked Mum for some new ones, but hadn't liked to.

'Can't be comfortable wearing a seven-year-old's wardrobe,' Masher grinned, before de-bagging a struggling Jake and flying his trousers up the school flagpole.

Poor Jake. Even Mouse and Floss couldn't save the day, not with Saliva Shreeve and Bunions Bootle holding them off. Jake had no other option but to wear his school jumper over his pants as he sprinted home, his legs thrust inside the arm holes. He'd never felt so humiliated in his life.

Jake had barely come through the front door though, when Mum marched him and Lewis into the living room and sat them on the settee.

'There's something I need to tell you,' she said.

Jake's head spun with the possibilities. More than anything he wanted to hear that Dad was feeling better. Or that Arnie had

called with a change of heart. But Jake knew neither of them could be true. The look on Mum's face said otherwise.

'It's about your dad, kind of. And about me too.'

Oh no, thought Jake. They weren't getting divorced, were they? It was happening to kids at school, reduced to seeing their dads only every third weekend, when they got dragged off to the lame Feathered Friend Owl Sanctuary just outside town. Jake couldn't stomach the thought of looking at six straggly birds in the name of fun, he just couldn't.

'You see, the . . . *problems* that Dad's had since America . . . '

'Grumpy Daddy,' said Lewis, which earned him an elbow from Jake.

'Well, it's not getting any easier, and although he's working, he's not earning enough to keep us afloat. And I know, Jake, that you need a new school uniform, and Lewis's bike is broken, and . . . well, we can't afford any of those things without more money coming in.'

'I'll get a paper round,' said Jake. He could put everything right. He had to make amends. Mum smiled. 'That's very kind of you, sweetheart, but a paper round isn't going to cover it.'

Jake deflated as Mum went on.

'No, I'm going back to work. It's not forever . . . just until Dad's cloud passes.'

'Where? Doing what?'

'I've got my old job back – as an air hostess.'

'Flying where?'

'Long haul. America, Canada, Australia maybe.'

This was disastrous news, thought Jake. 'Who's going to look after us?'

'Dad will help, when he's feeling up to it.'

Hang on. Dad was barely talking at the moment – how could he possibly look after the two of them *and* cook them dinner *and* read them stories?

'Plus,' added Mum, 'I've got some help lined up. From someone you already know.'

'Who?' Jake and Lewis asked.

'Lovely Enid Tinker from number eighty-eight.'

Jake's heart stopped in terror and distress.

There was nothing lovely about Enid Tinker, apart from the fact that she lived at the *far* end of the street. She was all false teeth and crocheted cardigans.

Jake thought quickly. 'Wouldn't it be easier if I looked after Lewis? You know, with Dad's help. Then we wouldn't have to bother Enid at all.'

Mum was having none of it. 'What sort of mum would I be if I left you in charge, eh? It's important Dad helps, but he needs some *adult* support too. So Enid will be here in the mornings and evenings after school, and at weekends, if your dad has to rest.'

Jake's mind raced.

He'd heard that Enid Tinker wasn't even human.

That she was a freak, a mutant, a science experiment gone horribly wrong. The kids of Storey Street called her Robo-Gran; at least, the kind ones did.

Things were going badly enough without adding her into the mix.

Jake wanted to scream, but what was the point? It was a done deal and there was no getting out of it.

23
'Dig For Victory!'

The door slammed shut and that was it, a week after breaking the terrible news, Mum had flown the nest. Well, sort of. Her plane was on a runway, fifty miles away, but you get the idea, don't you? Good, then we can crack on.

There were four long faces left in the hall. Mournful expressions from Jake, Lewis and Dad, all miserable about being abandoned. But Enid's face was the longest of them all. That's what a century of gravity did to you. She had the saggy skin of an African elephant: and a hide as thick too. (OK, she probably wasn't more than eighty, but she certainly looked it!)

'Right,' she boomed. 'Pick your faces off the floor and get yourselves dressed.'

Dad did his best to look as if he was still in charge by waving the boys up the stairs, before Enid got her (false) teeth into him too.

'You as well, my lad,' she said, clipping him around the ear.

'I don't have to be at work till ten-thirty,' he answered quietly. 'And I didn't sleep so well last night. Thought I'd go back to bed for a bit.'

'Not on your nelly!' she roared. 'If you need to sleep better, have a milky drink and a bath before bed. The sun's in the sky now, so you've no business being asleep.'

'But—'

'No buts! Do you think we had time to lie in our beds feeling maudlin during the war? No, we did not. We had to get up, face the day and DIG FOR VICTORY!'

Jake was listening to all this as he pulled on his starchy new school uniform. He had no idea what Enid was banging on about. He didn't know what year she'd been born in, but reckoned her birth certificate had been scratched onto a piece of slate or cave wall.

Dad unwisely decided to ignore her and climb back into bed, wedging a chair against the door. Enid merely saw this as a challenge and Jake sped out of the bathroom to see her banging repeatedly on it. After a minute or so, her fists were a blur – as if she really was a robot like the other kids had said! For a moment, Jake thought he could hear her whirring and fizzing, until he realised it was just her hearing aid playing up.

'George Melvin Biggs,' she roared. 'You might think you're the fighter round here, but I promise you, if you don't open the door this minute, I will rip it off its hinges and fashion it about your head!'

Jake gulped. He believed every word she said – he'd be stupid not to. But he also knew from recent experience that once Dad was in bed, there was nothing that could get him out of it. Not food, not wrestling, nothing.

So he did the decent thing and stepped into the firing line.

'Enid,' he crawled. 'Why don't you take us to school today? I'm sure Lewis would love to show you off to all his friends.'

What he really meant was: *Don't you dare come anywhere near anyone that knows me. Please!*

Luckily, it seemed to work, as Enid stopped hammering at Dad's (now severely dented) door.

'Right then. *I* shall take the boys to school,' she said. (She seemed to think it was suddenly her idea.) 'But I tell you this, George Biggs, I'll be back!'

Jake shivered at the prospect. She was terrifying. He made a note of that last line in his head.

Reckoned Floss could make use of it in one of her films.

Ten minutes later, Enid, Jake and Lewis were on the short walk to school when the lumpish frame of Masher Milner loomed into view. Jake knew that if he was spotted with Enid, then a whole new world of pain was about to unfold. But as Jake made to scarper to the safer company of Mouse and Floss, he was stopped by his teacher, Miss Maybury.

'No Mum today, Jake?' she said.

'No, Miss, she's working, on her way to Rio,' Jake replied.

Miss Maybury looked momentarily envious.

'What about your dad?'

'He's at home, in bed,' interrupted Enid.

'Under the weather,' added Jake quickly. 'Virus. Terrible business. Snot everywhere.' He couldn't help but defend Dad, even it was a bit of a lie.

Miss Maybury turned to Enid.

'Oh dear,' she said. 'I was rather banking on help from Lucie. You see, the school is trying to do something quite extraordinary. We're hoping to set a new world record, and we're asking for parent volunteers.'

'What an excellent idea,' said Enid. (Jake thought her false teeth might fly out in excitement.)

'Perhaps you could volunteer, Grandma?' asked Miss, which made Jake want to scream, 'SHE'S NOT RELATED TO ME! SHE WAS BORN IN A SCIENCE LAB!!'

'Oooh, no, not me,' said Enid. 'My record-breaking days have been over since I leaped over the Great Wall of China on a unicycle.'

What? Jake thought, though he couldn't dismiss the possibility entirely. Enid was certainly tough enough.

'Oh, that's such a shame,' said Miss Maybury. 'There's nothing better for the soul than being involved in a project like this. Does wonders for the confidence – and imagine being part of a world record team!'

A million light bulbs flashed in Jake's head. This was a perfect opportunity for Dad! Mum said he needed to be kept busy – and as for the confidence Miss was talking about? Well, Dad could do with an injection of the stuff.

The next words tumbled out of Jake's mouth before he could stop them.

'My dad will help.'

'Excellent,' said Miss Maybury, smiling.

'Super,' said Enid.

Everyone was happy.

Now all they had to do was persuade Dad.

The Record Breaker

Mum was delighted with Jake when she arrived home from Rio. She thought it was the best idea since a baker took a sharp knife to a large and unwieldy hunk of bread.

'You brilliant boy,' she said, hugging him tightly, before breaking the news to Dad.

'It'll do you good,' she said, as he pretended to watch the telly over her shoulder. 'The doctor said it was important to exercise. The fresh air will put hair on your chest.'

Jake was more concerned about putting flesh back on Dad's bones. He was still constantly putting treats in front of Dad, only to bin the untouched food hours later.

Dad's reaction wasn't as positive as Mum's. He mumbled something incoherent, until Mum suddenly turned the TV off.

'I don't feel up to it,' he moaned. He didn't *look* up to it either. He looked horrified, as if Mum had asked him to climb Everest in the nude.

'It's only one day, Dad,' Jake said. 'One Saturday. And I'll be there. It'll be like before, you and me on an adventure. Please.' He felt a twang of pain as he remembered how amazing their Saturdays together used to be.

Dad wasn't convinced and reached for the remote control again.

'They don't want me involved. I'll only mess it up,' he said.

Jake tried to imagine what was going through Dad's head. Did he *really* think he was that useless? Well, he wasn't having it, not when it wasn't true.

'Mess it up? It's perfect for you,' Jake said. 'They're trying to create the biggest domino rally ever.'

'That's right,' added Mum. 'You've spent years knocking down the ugliest buildings on the planet. A few million dominoes will be a breeze!'

'Can you really not do it, Lucie?'

'I can't. I'll be flying over the Bermuda Triangle.'

'Wish I was,' he sighed grimly. 'What about Enid?'

'She's at the hospital that day. Having something replaced.'

'Hopefully her personality,' Dad said.

'Ha!' Jake laughed. It was good to hear Dad joking.

'Mum's right. It's perfect for you. And you know, I'd love it if you were there. It'd be just like Saturdays used to be – special.'

'OK, I'll give it a go,' Dad said finally.

Jake dived into his arms and hugged him tighter than any wrestler ever dared. 'You're the best!' he yelled, feeling Dad hug back.

He'd done it. This was the first step back to a super-charged Dad.

Ten days later, Jake and Dad found themselves walking towards the school gates. Jake knew Dad was nervous. There was a slight tremor in his hand as he held it.

There was quite a crowd of volunteers gathered in the playground when they arrived, including a smarmy-looking Masher and his usual band of muppets, who Jake tried to ignore. There were plenty of folk who Dad knew and liked, like Mouse and Floss's parents. He listened as they tried to engage Dad in conversation.

'George!' they called affectionately. 'We haven't seen you in ages! Where've you been hiding? Under the bed?'

'Well . . . I . . . er . . . well . . .'

Come *on*, Jake thought impatiently, looking around the playground. The sooner Dad got to work, the better. Suddenly, his eyes fell on something that made his spirits soar – he'd found the perfect way for Dad to help.

Parked on the slope by the delivery entrance was a truck with its hazard lights flashing. And on the back of the truck were crates filled with piles and piles of white-spotted dominoes.

Jake made straight for Miss Maybury.

'Miss, Miss,' he said. 'It's going to take a strong man to lift all those crates off the truck. But my dad can do it. Then we can form a chain and pass them into position.'

Jake might have thought Dad looked like a stick insect lost in a rhino's wardrobe, but he was still the biggest parent there.

'Splendid,' his teacher said with a grin, waving them off in the truck's direction.

Within minutes, Dad worked himself into an impressive rhythm. Crate after crate of dominoes was plucked effortlessly from the truck and passed down the chain. Dad lifted them like they were matchboxes, when it took Jake, Floss AND Mouse to lift one on its own.

After a while, Dad paused. Not because he was tired, but because of the backlog he'd created.

Jake felt a surge of pride. It was working. It felt like being ringside again, as Dad-the-machine showed everyone his power and determination. Any second now, a victorious Dad would hoist Jake on his shoulders before the cheering crowd. He shook the image out of his head. No point getting carried away, not yet.

But then, because this is a story and there are still a handful of chapters to go, something did happen. Course it did. Did you think the rest of the pages were full of descriptions of flowers or something?

What happened was this:

The crate that Mouse, Floss and Jake were carrying was too heavy. They dropped it, spilling dominoes all over the tarmac. Kneeling to clear up, none of them spotted Masher Milner and Saliva Shreeve creep past them towards the truck's cab. With Masher on lookout, Saliva snuck into the driver's seat and released the handbrake, before the pair slunk quietly away.

The movement was slow at first, but not for long. When Dad turned to grab another crate, he found the truck wasn't there any more. It was now accelerating towards the growing domino alley and the group of unsuspecting volunteers only thirty metres away.

By the time Jake heard his dad's shout and turned, the ten-ton truck was practically upon them.

'MOOOOOOOOVE!' Jake yelled. Or it could've been something far ruder, a word no ten-year-old should know, never mind say. Either way, it was enough to get everyone's attention and have them scattering to safety. Unfortunately, the same couldn't be said of their painstaking domino preparation. Jake watched as the first few dominoes fanned outwards, only to be eaten alive by the back wheels of the truck. By the time the wheels stopped turning, every single domino had been knocked flat or crushed.

There were tears and shouts of disappointment.

'What on earth happened?' shrieked Miss Maybury, which gave Masher and Saliva the chance to execute their dastardly plan.

'He did it!' they said, pointing at Dad, who was doing his very best 'What, me?' face.

Jake looked at Dad, then at Masher, then back to Dad. He couldn't believe what he was hearing. This was ridiculous.

'We tried to stop him!' Masher yelled. 'But he was too strong.'

'He was mumbling,' added Saliva. 'We couldn't hear all of it cos he was rambling like a mad man . . .'

Jake felt his insides cooking as Masher continued:

'Then he climbed into the cab and took off the handbrake. He was smiling. Like he wanted to ruin everything.'

That was it. Jake lost his cool. He didn't care if he was about to get the beating of his life. No way Milner was saying those things about Dad and getting away with it.

He ran towards Masher, arms flailing, only for a strange thing to happen. Despite having the strength to overpower Jake in seconds, Masher didn't do anything. Instead, he let Jake pin him, before wailing loudly and pathetically.

'AAARRRGGHHHH! Get him off me. Look! Look! He's as dangerous as his dad. Ow, ow – he's hurting me!'

With that, it all kicked off. Parents waded in to separate the boys, and Jake was restrained by three burly dads. Fingers were pointed, voices were raised, louder and louder. George was utterly paralysed. He knew he hadn't released the brake, but then again, he'd been the only one near the truck, so he felt he should've done more to stop it. All he could see and hear was shouting and noise: all he could see were eyes and voices blaming him. Somehow, he'd done it again, messed everything up. He had to get out of there before he made things even worse.

It was Masher that spotted him, taking great delight in the execution of his plan. 'Look!' he yelled. 'He's running off! That proves it, everything I said.'

Jake struggled from the arms of his captors. He saw Dad tearing across the playground, through the school gates and up Storey Street.

And he was scared. Because now Dad was running, Jake worried he might not ever stop.

25

Sending Out An SOS

Dad was nowhere to be seen when Jake got home, though he was more worried about this than Enid, even after explaining the domino debacle.

'Maybe he's drowning his sorrows at the Stagger Inn,' she said. 'My Joseph stopped for a drink there every night on the way home from work. Never did him any harm.'

Jake frowned. He'd never heard about a Robo-Grandad before.

'Forty years we were married. Liver failure did for him in the end. Came from nowhere.' And with that she began scouring a frying pan with such ferocity that Jake thought he saw smoke coming off it.

What should he do now? He could hit the streets to look for Dad, though he didn't have a clue where he might have gone. Jake didn't like it, but all he could do was sit tight and wait for him to come home.

He tried to get comfy in Dad's chair. He put some wrestling DVDs on, but no matter how hard he tried, Jake just couldn't concentrate. His eye kept straying to the clock, and you know what they say about that, don't you? That's right, a watched clock never boils . . . or is it a watched pot that never does that? Oh, I don't know, I'm as worried about Dad as you and Jake are.

Four o'clock became five, which crawled to six, seven, eight and nine. Jake ate his supper without tasting a mouthful, and before he knew it, it was time for bed. He lay awake for ages, worrying about where Dad might be. Had the other parents believed Masher and tracked Dad down to shout at him? He wasn't sure Dad could take that right now.

Jake had no idea how long he lay there, stewing, but he was sure that as his eyes finally closed, he heard the call of a lonely, sole cockerel. His cry wasn't enough to keep Jake awake.

Jake woke on Sunday to light pouring through the curtains, jolting his mind back to yesterday's disaster. Without hesitation, he dashed into Mum and Dad's room, desperate to see a Dad-sized lump under the covers. There was nothing except an impeccably straight duvet and the sound of Enid snoring from the spare room.

Maybe he was up already, thought Jake, pounding down the stairs. But there was no trace of Dad downstairs either. No boots at the door, no empty teacup on the table, and certainly no trail of crumbs from the biscuit tin. He still hadn't come home.

Jake's panic levels went intergalactic. He couldn't listen to another lame excuse about the pub from Enid. No, if Dad wasn't home, well, he'd just have to go out and find him.

He pulled on his shoes and shut the front door quietly behind him. He rounded up Mouse first, then Floss, who were delighted to be woken up at seven o'clock on a Sunday morning. Almost as delighted as both sets of parents, who came to the door with the most spectacular cases of 'bed-head' Jake had ever witnessed.

'So you haven't seen him since he legged it yesterday?' asked Mouse, when Floss's parents had traipsed back to bed.

Jake shook his head.
Floss decided it was time to take control.
'OK, Mouse, you check the all the cafés in the old town. Maybe George got his appetite back,' she said.

Jake loved his friend's optimism, and had to hope it was well placed.

Mouse nodded. 'No worries. We'll find him.'

'And I'll cover the shopping centre and arcade, especially the food court on the top floor.'

'And I'll wait here till people get up,' said Jake. 'Ask if anyone's seen him.'

The threesome split up, agreeing to meet again an hour later.

But that sixty minutes proved fruitless, as did the next one, and the one after that.

Finally, the friends slumped on the sofa at The House That Was Stolen, racking their brains for more places they could try. Jake was terrified. What if Dad never came back?

'If we don't find him soon, I'll have to call the police,' Jake said.

'Don't you think you should call your mum first?' Floss said.

'She's halfway across the ocean,' wailed Jake. 'So her phone will be switched off. And I don't want her to arrive in Australia and hear bad news. No, I'll find him. I mean, he's got to be somewhere, hasn't he? But where would he go if he was feeling down?'

'Did you look in the fridge?' offered Mouse.

Jake wasn't listening, because he'd had an idea. He wasn't certain about it, but it had to be worth a go. 'Ugly Sisters!' he yelled.

'We were only trying to help!' said Mouse.

'No, you plank, the buildings Dad was going to knock down. They still haven't finished demolishing them. I know it's a long shot, but he might have gone there, to sit in his cab. He used to love being high above the ground, said it was the perfect place to think.'

Mouse jumped to his feet in full-on superhero mode.

'Then what are we waiting for? Let's do this!'

Neither Floss nor Jake needed any encouragement. The threesome sprinted towards the loving arms of the Ugly Sisters.

26

A Hug Like No Other . . .

Jake, Floss and Mouse didn't get a warm welcome from the Ugly Sisters – they were a couple of decrepit buildings after all. Mind you, if the Sisters *had* been alive, they probably would've given you the sort of slobbery kiss an ageing great aunt inflicts on you on your birthday.

The buildings loomed in front of them, and in their half-demolished state, looked more sinister than ever. So heinous and dangerous were they that the builders had erected a huge fifteen-metre fence, topped off with barbed wire.

'Can't see your dad climbing over that,' said Mouse. 'No matter how much weight he's lost.'

'He wouldn't need to. He had a key,' said Jake, spotting the padlock on the gate.

'Well, it's still locked, so he can't be here,' said Floss. She wasn't sure she liked the look of the place – it reminded her too much of the horror movies she'd made.

Jake wasn't leaving until he'd checked the crane's cab, though. He knew the chances of finding Dad here might be slim (especially after his last visit was such a disaster), but he was out of other ideas.

He started searching for a weak spot in the fence. Mouse spotted one ten minutes later – a small chink, just big enough for the three of them to crawl through.

Once inside, the semi-smashed buildings seemed to lean over them. The threesome scooted quickly to the relative safety of the crane's ladder.

'Can you see him?' asked Floss as Jake peered skywards.

He shrugged. 'Not from here. I'll have to climb up.'

Jake had never made the long journey to the cab alone before. He'd always had Dad behind him. But this wasn't the time to be cowardly, not if he wanted to find Dad. With shaking hands, Jake climbed rung after rung, feeling the wind nip at his arms and legs as the ground slid further and further away. By the time he reached the top, Jake's heart was hammering. He'd been rehearsing what to say all the way up – how he'd tell Dad that none of this was his fault – the big fight, the domino disaster, none of it. It had been Jake who'd constantly tried to shove Dad into the spotlight; so it was Jake's fault that everything had gone wrong. If it hadn't been for him, well, Dad would still be happily and anonymously destroying eyesores across the Seacross horizon.

But when he pulled himself through the cab's hatch, ready to pour his heart out, he found he was alone. Dad might be thinner now, but he definitely wasn't crouched behind the gear stick. The disappointment overwhelmed him and Jake slumped into the chair, head on the control panel, trying to force back tears.

Where on earth was he? Had he had an accident? Or run away? What would happen if Mum came home before he did? What would Jake say to her? He was meant to be making things better, to be looking after Dad, not driving him away.

'No joy?' asked Floss anxiously when Jake reached the ground.

'He'll turn up,' said Mouse unconvincingly. 'He might even be at home already, wondering where *you* are.'

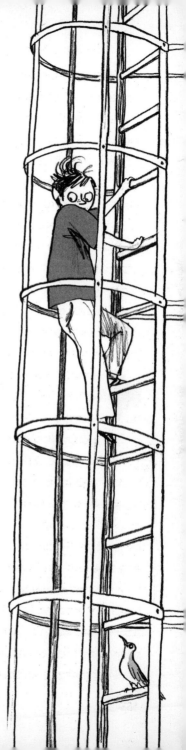

Jake doubted it. Dad didn't talk to Jake like he used to. Didn't realise he was even there most of the time. He could've painted himself blue and stuck pencils up his nose for the past month and Dad wouldn't have noticed. That said, there wasn't much eft for him to do except go home and see.

As Jake motioned his friends back towards the fence, he heard an odd noise behind them: an echoing, swirling wail that seemed to be coming from the heart of the ugliest Sister. There was a pain to it that was terrifying, yet impossible to run from.

'Did you hear that?' said Jake, stopping in his tracks.

'Only in my worst nightmares,' answered Mouse, shivering.

Floss didn't like it either. 'Probably just wind,' she said.

Mouse looked over his shoulder at her. 'Well, it wasn't me. I haven't eaten for hours.'

Jake ignored them. There was no way he was leaving until he knew what had made that sound. For all he knew, it could be Dad. What if he was trapped under a pile of rubble? He couldn't ignore it.

'It came from in there,' he said, pointing back towards the smashed-up door of one of the Sisters.

'Even more reason for us to leave,' said Mouse.

'But what if it's Dad?'

'You really think your dad, a demolition expert, would take one step inside a building that looks like it was built by the laziest of the three little pigs?' said Mouse, folding his arms.

Jake thought about it for a second. Normally, he'd have said no without hesitation. But Dad was acting so differently since he came back from Vegas – who knew what he would do?

'I don't know,' he said. 'So I don't have a choice.' And with that, he pulled open the door and disappeared into the building.

Jake and Floss looked at one another.

'How much do you *really* like Jake?' Mouse asked his friend.

Floss exhaled. 'An awful lot less than I did twenty seconds ago.'

'But too much for us to go and have an ice cream instead?'

Floss nodded, sighed again, and took Mouse's hand.

'Shall we?' she said.

And in they went.

27

Darker Than Darker Than Dark...

There are certain things that people tell you never to do.

Like eat yellow snow. Or offer a piggyback to a ravenous grizzly bear.

Or (because there's neither snow nor a bear in this story) step inside a semi-demolished building, regardless of whether or not you have a missing dad.

But Jake, Floss and Mouse were on a mission. It was just a shame that they'd chosen a mission inside something so dark.

'What are we doing? This is SUCH a bad idea,' hissed Mouse, all superhero bravado left at the door.

'SSSSHHHH!'

'I heard something.'

'Probably the building, wanting to be put out of its misery,' said Floss.

'Don't say that,' said Mouse. 'Not while we're standing inside it.'

Jake was scared too. But he had to be sure it wasn't Dad in there.

'All I want to do is check it out. Two minutes and we'll go, I promise.'

Jake stumbled on. The noise came again, still in front of them.

It was louder this time, closer. Whether it was animal, human or spectral, it was a cry full of pain and suffering.

'Dad?' Jake whimpered. 'Dad, if that's you, come out. I'm sorry about what happened. It was all my fault. We're here to take you home. The kettle's on and everything . . .'

Another howl pierced the air, and another. It was much closer now. The friends pushed themselves against a damp wall. Jake saw a pair of eyes flickering in the dark, edging closer.

Suddenly a dirty, fear-filled dog skittered between their legs, spitting up dust and debris behind it.

'AAAARRRGHHH!' they wailed.

Their panicked voices made the dog worse. It howled louder, the sound bouncing from wall to wall. Jake felt ridiculous. How could he have mistaken a dog for his dad?

Things start to crumble and crash around them. Feelings of stupidity changed quickly into sheer, undiluted terror.

'What was that falling?' he yelled. 'A table? A wardrobe?'

'No way!' Mouse screamed. 'Sounded more like the ceiling. We need to get out of here – quick!'

The dog, as if it had understood, bolted towards the exit, but as they followed, Jake felt the floor below them quake, rumble and tilt, and then an avalanche of rubble was falling, falling, falling and everything went dark, dark, dark.

'You OK?' Jake whispered, as soon as he dared. Nothing was

bruised, but he still hurt. Little wonder, given what he'd led them into.

'Did that really happen?'

'Do you mean, did the ceiling just cave in and bury us alive? Cos, yeah,' said Mouse, sounding panicky, 'clearly it did.'

'Keep your voice down,' hissed Floss. 'If the walls are crumbling, the last thing we need is you shouting. Now, think. We have to try and get word to people. Tell them what's happened.'

Thank goodness for Floss, thought Jake.

'Can you get a signal on your phone?' he asked, staring at his mobile. 'I've got nothing.'

Mouse shook his head. 'My battery's dead.'

'One bar!' Floss whispered excitedly. 'A signal. I've got a signal!'

'Then use it!' said Mouse, who already needed a wee, but didn't think this was the time to mention it.

Floss called home, starting the conversation with, 'Dad, you're not going to believe this, and please stay calm, but . . .' Not that her dad did stay calm. How could he? As Jake listened to Floss explain, he wanted to kick himself. How many times had Dad warned him, *Never play on building sites*? Yet here they were, trapped inside, possibly about to be crushed, because he'd been stupid enough to ignore that advice. He'd have screamed in frustration if the walls weren't so fragile.

While they waited for help to arrive, Jake paced the room. Well, kind of. It wasn't easy or safe to walk anywhere when it was so dark. He sort of shuffled from foot to foot instead.

'I've got to get us out of here,' he repeated over and over again.

'Really, Sherlock?' said Mouse. 'I hadn't thought of that.'

'No, I mean, I've got to find Dad. This was the last place he could have been. And if he's not here, then . . . then . . .'

'Then what?' said Floss.

'I don't know. He must have left Seacross, mustn't he? He must be really angry with me, and maybe . . . maybe he's never coming back!'

'But why would he be angry with you?'

'Because everything that's happened in the last few months has all been because of me. I put him in the one thing he didn't want – the spotlight. I should have left him alone. We should've carried on fighting vicars and clowns, That should've been enough. He was still my dad, he was still the best. And now I can't even tell him that because he's gone, I'm in here and he's never coming back!'

There was silence in the dark then, as they all faced the seriousness of their predicament. Only Floss dared to break the quiet.

'You *can* tell him, you know.'

'No I can't,' whispered Jake. 'There's nothing, nothing I can do.'

'Au contraire,' Floss added, which annoyed Jake. She knew he couldn't speak Spanish.

He didn't stay mad long, though, as a flash of light lit up the room. Floss was pointing her camera at his face.

'Say that again,' she smiled. 'Exactly what you just said. And I'll make sure it reaches your dad. I promise.'

28
Dad Goes Viral...

It didn't take long for word to get out.

Thirty-eight minutes had passed since Floss had called her dad, and already there was a crowd at the demolition site gate.

'Have you heard?' whispered one man to the next. 'There's three kiddies trapped inside. Been in there four days already!'

'Three kids?' frowned his neighbour. 'I heard it was a whole class. Took a wrong turn on a geography field trip a week ago.'

A third man scoffed. 'You two know nothing. There's a family stuck inside them walls. Followed a treasure map, they did, and discovered a trunk of gold when the curse guarding it struck.'

It was a shame Jake and Mouse couldn't hear these tales as they got more and more outlandish. It would have kept their minds off the fact they were trapped inside a building that had less chance of staying upright than a snowman in the Sahara Desert.

Floss was too busy to listen to idle tittle-tattle – she was editing Jake's message for Dad.

'Does it really need fiddling with?' Jake asked impatiently. 'I thought the idea was to get it on the internet as quickly as possible, before Dad gets too far away.'

'You know, you could try being grateful. If I didn't have this kit on my phone then you'd still be leaving messages on a phone that your dad clearly doesn't have switched on. One more minute and I'll post it on YouTube. Then all I have to do is text the police. They'll pass the web address on to the media and *voilà*, everyone will see it. Won't be long till your dad comes running home.'

That should've made Jake feel happier, but it didn't. Not really. What if Dad saw the video and *still* didn't come back? It was hard to find a silver lining in this dark room. Especially when it could collapse at any minute.

Out in the sunshine, *Operation Oh My Goodness, This Is Fraught With Danger* was moving through the gears. The police had arrived, along with a builder, a physicist, and a HUGE fish and chip van (lugging endless amounts of rubble made for many empty stomachs).

The police were nervous, knowing full well they were involved in the most dangerous game of Jenga imaginable. What they really needed was someone who knew the process of demolition back to front and upside down. Someone who could take one look at the Ugly Sister and tell them which brick to pluck and which to leave alone.

But when they spoke to George's boss, he only came up with one name. The best in the business: George Biggs.

The trouble was, George was nowhere to be found. So when they received Floss's video link, they immediately forwarded it to every TV and radio station in the country, complete with a plea of their own, demanding they play it on a continuous loop.

As the policeman hit send, the Ugly Sister threw another huge tantrum, dislodging three tons of masonry from its upper walls, down on the floor below.

Wherever George Biggs was, they all had to hope and pray that someone would recognise him. Seacross needed him. And they needed him now.

29

Fresh from the Kebab Shop . . .

George Biggs was not in a good place, mentally *or* geographically. But let's start with his mood first. He was in a terrible state – feeling sad, mournful and utterly, utterly useless.

Everything he touched, it seemed, turned to dust. Even the stuff he was good at, like wrestling. He shuddered as he remembered that night in Las Vegas. He'd had his chance and blown it. He could imagine the disappointment on Jake's face as he watched it on the giant screen, his dreams disappearing in a flash. And since then? Well, he hadn't been able to do anything right. He wasn't sleeping properly, but he couldn't get up either. When people spoke, their words didn't make sense, nor could they understand what was happening to him. How could they when he didn't understand it either?

He couldn't even swing a wrecking ball any more. He had to watch as Lucie went back to work. How could Jake look up to him when he was failing at everything? Maybe the only thing left for him to do was the thing that would break his heart – leave.

It didn't have to be for ever, just until he shook off this cloud. Maybe he'd find somewhere new for them to live, somewhere they could start afresh, where nobody knew them. Maybe, he thought sadly, they were actually better off without him. He had a lot of decisions to make.

His surroundings were just as miserable. George was slumped in a kebab shop. And not just any kebab shop; the world's worst kebab shop. Sam 'n' Ella's Kebab Wonderland, which sat by Seacross train station.

No sober or sane person ever bought anything there. Not if they valued their stomach linings and favoured life over a prolonged, painful and windy death. So it said a lot about George's mood that he was sitting (as their only customer that week) wading through a deluxe Empire State Kebab. (At least, that's what the menu said it was.)

George didn't care. He hadn't tasted anything he'd eaten since that fateful night in Las Vegas. He wasn't hungry now either. He just felt he deserved to spend the next seventy-two hours with the world's worst belly ache. So he tucked in as if he was eating a five-star banquet.

It was during his 473rd mouthful (this was an Empire State Kebab after all) that something caught his eye. At first he dismissed it, thinking the out-of-date meat was rotting his brain. But when he looked again, he saw it was real. There, on the black-and-white TV on the counter, was his son, talking straight into the camera, and at the top of the screen was a rolling caption which read:

Son Trapped in Derelict Building Appeals to Dad to Come Home.

'Sweet mercy!' Dad yelled, pushing the table and his food to the floor (the floor started smoking as the meat burned the varnish from it). 'Turn that up, will you? That's my boy on there!'

The guy behind the counter (I think it was a man, as Sam and Ella both had moustaches) fought with the volume control, and Jake's wobbly voice filled his dad's ears.

'I'm begging you, Dad, wherever you are, please come home. I need you. I need to tell you I'm sorry, that I never should have got you into wrestling in the first place, never mind making

BREAKING NEWS

you do it in front of the whole world. I did it for all the wrong reasons. I did it for me instead of you, and I wish I hadn't. I promise not to mention wrestling ever again, honest. I'm just so sorry. Please come home, Dad. Please?'

Dad's head spun faster than a tumble dryer in a tornado. He couldn't believe what was happening, but he did know he had to do something about it. So with great athleticism (for a man who'd just eaten a rancid kebab), he sprinted for the door. There wasn't a millisecond to lose.

The sun was setting. It had flexed its muscles for as long as it could, but now its fading light threw long shadows across the demolition site.

The past five hours had proved fruitless. For every brick that was taken away, another three seemed to fall in its place. The rescue crew hadn't been able to pass food or water inside, and by now the kids' mobile phones had run out of juice. No one knew if the buildings would last the night in their fragile state. Nerves were shredded, morale was low.

But just as hope was beginning to leave along with the daylight, a final shadow was cast upon the Ugly Sisters' skirt. It was long and distorted, and there was an authority about it that had people parting to let it through.

'Don't touch that!!' a voice yelled. 'And move away from that pillar. In fact, do nothing, say nothing and touch nothing unless I say so.'

Standing there, surveying the damage, was George Biggs.

Inside he was trembling, terrified that he could mess things up again. But he couldn't let that show. After all, this was HIS domain, and it was HIS son stuck inside. He had a job to do.

'I'm the Demolition Man,' he roared. 'So stand back and let me work.'

30

Lower Than...

Morale in the belly of the Ugly Sister was lower than an ant's undercarriage.

They'd been trapped for over twelve hours now, and Jake was consumed by guilt. What had he been thinking, leading his friends here? Every time he heard a noise, he was afraid the building was about to come crashing down around them and that would be it. He thought about Mum and Dad, and how

awful it would be to never hear their laughs or experience the warmth of their hugs. What if Dad never put him in a headlock again or hoisted him effortlessly onto his shoulders and up to bed?

'Is your battery definitely dead?' Jake asked Floss for the fifteenth time.

'Why? Do you want to eat it or something?' Floss replied grumpily.

'No, I just can't stand the waiting. Or the feeling that all this is my fault.'

'No point in beating yourself up. Let's play a game to take our minds off it,' said Mouse. 'I'll give you two options and you have to pick the best one.'

Neither Jake nor Floss had the energy to say no, so Mouse ploughed on.

'Superman or Spiderman?'

'Are we talking about the designs on your underpants or just in general?' said Jake. He knew any game from Mouse would involve superheroes, but at least he was trying to stop them all worrying.

'Very funny. I'm not *completely* obsessed with superheroes, you know.'

'Yeah, right. Prove it.'

'OK, I will.'

There was silence as Mouse thought hard about a different subject.

'Iron Man or Batman?'

Floss groaned. 'See? You're *obsessed!*'

'But that's where you're wrong, because Iron Man and Batman

aren't superheroes. They're vigilantes with no special powers. They are multi-billionaires with the financial clout to create armour that sustains their vigilante status.'

That was it for Floss. Hunger had kicked in and she had three choices:

1. Eat Mouse to shut him up,

2. Use his head as a battering ram to escape,

or

3. Give him a piece of her mind.

'Have you ever listened to yourself, Mouse? Have you ever imagined, for one second, that neither of us give a monkey's about the difference between a superhero and a vigilante? Honestly, you're as bad as Jake banging on about the wrestling. What is it with you boys? We're trapped here, and we might never get out, especially if you keep using your excuse for a brain for such nonsense!'

It was an impassioned speech that saw Mouse and Jake fall into silence.

It didn't last long.

'Did you hear that?' said Jake suddenly.

'What?'

'That!'

'What, the echo of Mouse's stupidity?'

'No . . . well, there is that, of course, but this is something else. Listen.'

Ears were pricked and expectant. Was help finally on the way?

'I can't hear anything . . .'

'SSSSHHHH!'

And there it was again – a scratching noise.

'It's probably that stupid dog trapped in the next room . . .'

Jake didn't think it was, though. He thought it sounded like . . . He listened hard but the noise had stopped.

Silence.

The worst sound in the world.

Jake was having the most wonderful dream. Dad was back in Vegas, in full Demolition Man gear, ready for a rematch with the Tsunami Terror.

And this time, Dad was showing everyone what he was made of. With every body slam, the foundations of the auditorium vibrated, and the Terror's eyes spun in his head, begging for mercy. Finally, Dad pulled his opponent to his feet and with a slick, final flourish he unleashed the Wrecking Ball. The crowd went wild! They clapped so loudly the room shook . . .

And suddenly Jake was awake, to find no Vegas, no Dad, but the same trembling walls.

'Mouse? Floss?' he cried. 'I don't like this. Something's happening!'

Was this it? Was the Ugly Sister giving up? Jake's panic threw Mum, Dad and Lewis into his head in a jumble of memories. Days at the beach, birthday parties, smiles upon smiles upon smiles.

He pulled his friends close in a final act of solidarity.

'It'll be OK,' yelled Floss. 'It'll pass, just like the others . . .'

'Will it?' cried Mouse. 'Do you promise?' He'd never felt less like a superhero in his life.

Jake tried to think of something to say, something profound, or moving, or anything that wasn't a stream of petrified nonsense. But all he could think of was . . .

'Spiderman and Batman!'

'What?' yelled the other two.

'The best superhero and vigilante. I never liked Superman. He always seemed too good to be true.'

Mouse burst into tears and squeezed even harder. Floss followed suit. Even in the worst situation imaginable, they faced it together.

A further tremor rocked them backwards, but it didn't come from above, but from the wall to their left.

'This is it!' screamed Jake, as bricks started to crumble onto their feet.

There was a crash, a mushroom cloud of smoke, and then a blinding flash of light. For a moment Jake thought he might be dead. He'd heard heaven was supposed to be full of bright lights, but he'd never imagined that God would have torches strapped to every centimetre of his body.

'Jake?' God yelled, before breaking into a coughing fit.

Jake gasped as he squinted into the blinding light. Not daring to believe it, he reached out his hands and found a nose, cheeks and a chin. The face was thinner than it used to be, but there was no mistaking who it belonged to.

'DAD!'

31

The Great Escape

Jake squeezed Dad tightly. 'I'm sorry, I'm sorry, I'm sorry,' he cried.

'It's all right,' Dad said. 'Well, it will be if you let go of my throat. We haven't got much time. Follow me slowly. And touch nothing.'

With the precision of a surgeon, George cleared enough bricks for them to slither through. He'd moved so much masonry now that one false move could send the Ugly Sister into a monumental, final rage.

Centimetre by centimetre, they edged forward on their bellies like snakes and, after what felt like an endless journey, Mouse saw a bolt of light that wasn't coming from George's torches. It was coming from outside!

'We're nearly there!' he panted. 'I can see it. I can see the sun coming up.'

'Ssshhh and slow down,' hushed Dad. 'Take your time and keep your elbows tucked in.'

They did as they were told, arms shaking with cramp as they shuffled closer, not daring to stand, even when their toes were a metre clear of the doorway. The crowd looked on, not daring to breathe out.

Finally Dad clambered to his feet, and pulled Jake, Mouse and Floss into his embrace.

The people of Seacross went nuts. Jake was crying and he didn't care who saw it. Floss was too. Mouse yelled in pure delight.

The collective din, though, was too overwhelming for the Ugly Sister's eardrums, causing it to finally throw all of its toys clean out of the pram. Suddenly bricks were falling like missiles from the sky. The police and rescue squads sprinted back towards the gates. Dad scooped each of the kids into his arms and ran with every bit of strength he had left.

But had he made it? Had he managed to get the kids to safety? Nobody seemed to know. Dust and dirt engulfed the scene. It felt as if the world had ended.

The crowd waited, squinting as the dust finally cleared to reveal rubble. Endless piles of it.

'Can you see them?' one man cried.

'No!' called another. 'They must have been buried alive.'

Heads dropped. How could this be happening when George had come so close?

Only then, suddenly, there was a ripple of dust about thirty metres from where the building had stood. A small, yet significant, disturbance.

As one, the rescue team bolted towards it and, with scrabbling hands, began to pull the rubble away. On and on they dug, until they hit something. A tattered T-shirt. More rubble disappeared, to reveal a pair of jeans with a crescent of bum cheek popping out of the top, then a bald head and a pair of steel-capped boots.

The body wasn't moving.

Suddenly, the back spasmed and a cough echoed through the site. With a groan, the body bent at the waist. And there George Biggs stood, with three dusty, coughing figures clamped to him, still wrapped in the big man's arms. They were bruised, battered and scared, but they were alive – and all thanks to the bravery and bulk of one great man.

Jake opened his eyes to find his dad looking at him tearfully.

'It's OK, Dad,' Jake said. 'You did it.'

Tenderly, Dad set Floss and Mouse on their feet and watched as they went haring off through the gates towards their parents.

Jake, however, wasn't going anywhere. He attached himself

like a limpet with abandonment issues to Dad's chest. Not that George minded.

'I'm sorry, Dad,' Jake said, trying not to cry.

'Shush now,' Dad said. 'I saw you on the news already – you don't need to say it again. Not till I've said it too. All right?'

'All right,' Jake said, smiling, as his ears filled with the most unintelligible noise from the crowd. 'What are they shouting, Dad?'

Father and son turned to face a sea of clapping hands and a chorus of joyful chanting.

Jake took extra special pleasure from seeing Masher in the middle of the throng. His mouth was hanging open, utterly speechless.

Try and call my dad a chicken NOW, Jake thought, laughing to himself.

Then, something strange and wonderful happened.

Dad's lips curled upwards instead of down and he laughed, long and hard.

'Can you hear what they're singing, Jake? Listen!'

Jake felt his own grin form as the words fell into place.

They couldn't be chanting that, could they? Really?

Dad bent down and lifted Jake high onto his shoulders, just as he had done countless times before, in the middle of the wrestling ring.

But people weren't booing Dad now, and they weren't throwing things at him either. Not beer bottles, false teeth or cold slices of pizza. Oh no, the crowd were united with a simple cry: two words, but the best two words Jake had ever heard in his life.

'Demolition Man,' they chanted.

'Demolition Man, Demolition Man, Demolition Man!'

32

The End . . .

Well, nearly.

There are still a few bits and bobs to tie up; a few facts to clarify that must be itching your head like a scalp-full of lice.

What happened next? I hear you cry.

Did the cloud over Dad's head finally blow away?

Did Jake and Dad go back to being best mates?

Did Mum ever grab that flight to the moon?

Well, dearest reader, feast your eyes on this . . .

George Biggs sat at the dining table, the remnants of a mighty breakfast feast laid out in front of him. With great delight, he burped. It was fair to say that he'd eaten his share of bacon, sausage, eggs, beans, toast, black pudding and tomatoes, and he wasn't the only one. Everybody had a hunger that morning. Mum, Lewis, Jake and even Enid.

'Very nice, George Biggs,' the old lady said. 'You cooked up quite a storm there. I'll wash up.'

'No, you won't,' Dad said, heaving his gut from behind the

table. 'That's my job, though I can't promise not to lick the plates clean.'

Mum laughed. Her eyes sparkled with affection. 'Speaking of jobs,' she said. 'I'd better get going. Rio doesn't wait for anyone, you know, not even me.'

The boys rushed to hug her, but they weren't sad. Nine months had passed since she'd returned to work and they were used to her disappearing. They were used to Dad being at college too. It was better than him coming home from demolition sites tired and covered in dust. And WAY better than him endlessly moping his way round the house.

They were even used to Enid being around too – she was almost part of the family. She looked after the boys while Dad was in his classes and Mum was away.

There were a lot more smiles in the Biggs household these days. And it thrilled Jake to see Dad doing a lot of it. Learning to

be an architect filled George with joy, and Mum always returned from work wearing a bigger grin than the one she left with. She would bring a gift too. Not a tacky toy or souvenir; something way cooler. New stories all about the places she'd visited and the things she'd seen.

Now, after waving Mum off, Jake and Dad turned their attention to the kitchen. Jake piled the dirty plates into the sink and Dad pulled a long pair of rubber gloves over his chubby fingers. They reminded Jake of Dad's old wrestling costume and it made him smile. He didn't say anything, though.

There were a few things that Dad didn't ever talk about, including his heroics inside the Ugly Sister, which had seen him branded a hero.

Seacross Council had wanted to erect a statue to celebrate his bravery, but Dad wouldn't have it. They offered him a party instead, but Dad told them he was too busy with his family to

attend. News crews from around the country descended once more. But Dad had had enough of fame. Nosy reporters were turned away at the front door by a determined Jake. No one spoke to his Dad without HIS permission.

In the end, the council sent him a reward – buckets and buckets of loose change, collected by residents in awe of his deeds.

'I know just what to do with this,' Dad had said with a smile, before quitting his job and enrolling on an architecture course.

'From this point on, no more demolishing. Only building!'

Jake felt so proud. He definitely preferred his happy, anonymous dad to the famous, miserable one.

Funny how things work out, he thought, as he and Dad cleared and scrubbed and scoured. They chatted happily about this and that, though wrestling was never far from Jake's mind. He didn't watch *WOW!* any more; couldn't trust himself to not throw something at the screen whenever Arnie McBride slimed into view. But he did miss Saturdays with Dad.

'What time are you off to college?' he asked as Dad peeled the gloves off.

'Before you leave for school.'

'I don't mind getting there early. Enid can take Lewis. I'd rather walk with you.'

'Magic,' said Dad.

It had been a gloomy start to the day, but as the pair closed the door, the clouds parted and a ray of sunlight lit the length of Storey Street. Up the road Jake saw the looming figure of Masher Milner. The two boys locked eyes, but not for long, as the bully dropped his gaze sheepishly and scuttled off in the other direction.

'Turned out nice again,' Dad said.

Jake couldn't disagree, and wanted to save this moment up. Another five minutes and they'd part at the school gates.

'What are you doing today, Dad?' he asked.

'Examining concrete,' Dad replied, sounding genuinely excited about it.

'You're still enjoying it, then, the course?'

'Best thing I ever did – well, almost. Designing buildings is WAY better than knocking them down.'

Jake thought about what Dad said, and couldn't help himself. 'You know, you were pretty good at demolishing things. Don't forget that.'

'Ha. Buildings or people?'

'Both! But the people bit was more fun to watch.'

Dad looked at his son. He wasn't daft. He knew what wrestling meant to the boy.

'You miss it, don't you?'

Jake shrugged.

'We could still watch it, you know,' Dad said.

Jake's ears pricked up. 'Not WOW! No way.'

'Well, we could watch the stuff from Australia or Canada. When Mum's at work.'

'That would be great!' Jake said, beaming. He still thought about that night in Vegas and what could've been if Arnie McBride hadn't meddled like he had.

'Do you ever miss it, Dad?' Jake didn't mean to ask the question. It just slipped out.

'Bits of it,' Dad said. 'Travelling in the van with you, that moment before I came through the curtains—'

'Picking false teeth off your bum cheeks?'

'Always,' Dad said, laughing. 'Though I wonder if that whole Demolition Man thing was getting a bit tired. Whether Arnie was right to change things up.'

'Are you kidding? You walked to the ring with a raven on your shoulder. How was that possibly a good idea?'

'Fair enough,' said Dad. 'But if you *had* to change my wrestling name, what would you choose instead?'

Jake thought about it long and hard. Why change perfection? But he knew he had to give Dad something.

He looked up at him. Dad had put some bulk back on and was almost at fighting weight again. He looked smarter too. His hair and beard were cut shorter. He wore an ironed shirt and trousers and carried a briefcase. He looked every inch the architect he was training to be. And it gave Jake an idea.

'You know, we could flip the whole Demolition thing on its head.' Jake felt his pulse quicken. 'You could be The Architect of Anarchy! You could carry a blueprint into the ring every time you fight. We could scare opponents by saying they were plans for their downfall.'

Jake wasn't breathing. He didn't need or want to. He was on a roll.

'We could design you a new costume, keep the tie – you could use it to choke people!! We should use the briefcase too. Hide a breezeblock inside, so every time you swing it at someone's chin, it knocks them for six! Hhhhhm, we'd need a finishing move, though, something to equal The Wrecking Ball.

What do you think?'

He looked up, suddenly worried he'd gone too far.

Dad didn't look cross, or even mildly upset.

'It *could* work, couldn't it, Dad?' said Jake tentatively.

Dad put his briefcase into his other hand, and wrapped an arm around Jake.

'It could work, son,' he said. 'It could.'

Jake's heart flipped like it had been body-slammed. It felt magnificent.

Dad hadn't said yes. But he hadn't said no either. And that would do, for now.

(Not) The End...

Bodyslams and Thanks ...

I've had a right laugh writing this book, and was helped along the way by the following smashing folk;

Wrestlemaniacs Laura Dockrill and Daniel, David 'Crusher' O'Callaghan, David 'The Monster' Maybury, 'The Colossus' Shannon Cullen, Jason 'The Bomber' Bootle, 'Ten Foot Tall' Phil Carroll, Louise 'Eighth Wonder' Ward, 'The Bodyslamming' Booksellers Crow, my agent Jodie 'Headlock' Hodges, Jane 'Whiplash' Willis and Julian 'Dynamite' Dickson.

HUGE thanks also to everyone at Orion Children's Books, in particular to my editor, Jenny 'The Red Pen' Glencross, 'The Kingpin' Fiona Kennedy, Alex 'The Assassin' Nicholas, 'The Negotiator' Nina Douglas, Jo 'Raging Bull' Rose, Lisa 'MD' Milton, 'The Big Boo' Jack Milton-Herron, Paul 'The Legend' Litherland and 'The Duchess' Hermione Lawton.

Big ups also to 'The Hero' Abi Hartshorne, Sue 'Hard to spell' Michniewicz and Jane 'The Stickler' Sturrock.

I also owe a huge debt to Sara 'The Sensation' Ogilvie, whose work I have admired for years. I feel stupidly lucky to be working with you, mate. Thanks again for bringing Storey Street to life.

It's important for me to also thank two people who lit a fire under my imagination as a kid. John Godber, whose plays taught me there is wonderful drama to be found in the everyday, and the peerless Janet Doherty. Everyone should have a teacher like Miss D in their life, and I feel blessed that I did.

Bearhugs and headlocks also to my mum (the next one's for you), my friends in the Palace of Power and beyond, and of course, as always, my tag team partners, Laura, Albie, Elsie and Stan, who clothesline me with wonder, every single day.

Crystal Palace,
December 2014

the orion star

Sign up for **the orion star** newsletter to get inside information about your favourite children's authors as well as exclusive competitions and early reading copy giveaways.

www.orionbooks.co.uk/newsletters

Follow on

Orion
Children's Books